Laughing Humans
A Science Fiction Romance

Evelyn Rainey

ISBN: 0692518908
ISBN-13: 978-0692518908

Portals Publishing
An imprint of Denouement Literary Agency, LLC
PO Box 973, Eagle Lake, FL 33839

PortalsPublishing.com
DenouementLit.com

DEDICATION

To Jeanne Raulerson and Alice Gaines, thank you for your friendship and kindness and so many things.

CONTENTS

Chapter One
Bicanthra III

Professor Nobeha led his students into the observation room. Their hooves clopped hollowly against the tile floor. At four foot, eight inches, Nobeha was taller than most of his contemporaries. But now, in his ninth decade, the professor limped on his front right leg, the hair behind his ears was strikingly silver, and he habitually rubbed his hands together to keep them warm. Nobeha still enjoyed watching the back legs of his female students, though, and knew how to grade accordingly.

Today, he was lecturing his students on the troop of humans on this preservation.

"First discovered by the famous explorer Ward Ribbot around 1275 I.A. (that's four hundred years ago, for those of you yet to take the History of the Industrial Age), Laughing Humans became popular as pets of the royalty. They were quickly and easily trained to do menial tasks. They were also considered a delicacy. They were prolific when kept in groups, but died quickly when isolated. Once domesticated, they have great difficulty surviving when they are returned to the wild." His glance frosted a young woman who whispered how cute they were.

"After a century of scientific experimentation, we have reason to believe humans evolved of and by themselves. Their DNA bares no resemblance, past or present, to any other species on our planet."

"Professor Nobeha," interrupted Temos Tarscent (of the Tarscent Chair for Academics – there was no way was this Bicanth going to fail Nobeha's class!) "What is your opinion of Dr. Munsi Arton's theory that the Laughing Humans are actually aliens from another world?"

"I read his theory. I was buying groceries when I noticed the article. It was right next to the one by the woman who claims to have given birth to a

Sphardiclarkin. I thought they both had equal merit."

The room rippled with laughter.

"They're so quiet. Don't they ever make a noise?"
A young woman looked beseechingly at Nobeha.

"I'm told that -- in the wild -- their laughter could
be heard for miles. But in captivity, they rarely laugh.
However, your Dr. Arton has recorded several
episodes."

"I read that they permit themselves to make noise
only during childbirth and after the death of one of
their own kind." The speaker was a quiet student whose
name Nobeha could not remember.

"Permit themselves?!" Nobeha's anger flashed.
The lining of his ears turned blood red. "You believe
them capable of self-awareness?"

"I have read of experiments that were done
about fifty years ago. The report stated the Laughing
Humans have vocal chords and the ability to speak.
The scientists raised an infant, isolated from other
humans, and taught it to speak."

"And when they returned the infant to its troop?"
Professor Nobeha had the young man trembling.

"They -- the humans killed it."

"Your Dr. Arton stated at that time the Laughing

Humans viewed speech as a taboo. They killed their own because it spoke."

"They do make a cooing noise until they begin to walk." The woman commented.

"Evidence," the word bore all the prejudice and blood of science. "Evidence has proven the Laughing Humans are not intelligent enough to form the cooing into a coherent language. It is an evolutionary forerunner, perhaps. The animals killed the trained infant purely from instinct. It was different. Survival depends on cooperation. Enigmas must be dealt with."

"Are these really the last Laughing Humans in the world?" The woman did have the nicest shape between her front and back legs.

"Sadly enough, yes. Industrial wastes contaminated the rivers of their mountain habitat, by way of acid rain. When their numbers began diminishing, a campaign was started to save them. Most of them were rounded up and placed on preservations such as this one."

"And zoos," an indistinguishable voice from the back of the crowd commented.

"Yes, zoos." Silence. "Those humans died quickly. They seemed to develop a depressed, lethargic state, sometimes followed by dementia. Some were said to laugh constantly."

The class studied the troop in silence.

"Now look at that one. She is the last of her species. The one with red fur. We call her Hunter Rogue."

"She's the one that escapes all the time!" The young woman smiled at him.

"She has the widest territory of her kind. She's been found in each of the different biostations here. She was about ten years old when she first escaped. That was twenty years ago. The park went to great lengths to return her to her troop. The more we kept her in, the more determined she became. She is probably the most intelligent Laughing Human we've ever studied."

"With all the advances in biotechnology, why can't we breed her? Surely of all of them, she's the most rare." Temos, like the family he belonged to, always looked for the monetary value in things.

"Artificial insemination has been very successful. However, their hierarchy -- or 'pecking order' for those of you who did not read the chapter -- is followed by all to the death. Only certain females are allowed mates.

Any infant born to an unmated female is killed at birth. Oftentimes, offspring die of malnutrition. We have taken young females away from expectant mothers to improve the chance of the newborn. But there again, isolated Laughing Humans have a peculiarly high mortality rate, and we lose most of them within the first year. The males are becoming extremely rare. There has not been a male born in thirty-five years. With only the five males left, inbreeding may become a problem."

"So poor little Hunter Rogue can't have a mate and without one, her babies would be killed." The woman undoubtedly had a 'Save the Humans' bumper sticker on her vehicle. "Why can't you put her in a special cage and breed her there?"

"Special cages take special funding," Temos reminded the students.

"Bicanthra III, Bicanthra III. This is Earth Alliance probe T95S. Bicanthra III, this is Earth Alliance probe T95S. Answering your distress beacon. Do you copy?"

"I don't know, Bates. That beacon's got to be a couple hundred years old. Do you really think anyone's down there?"

Bates was eating a banana and spoke around a mouthful. "Microstellar dating has the beacon around five hundred years old. That was at the birth of Earth colonization. Seems to me we're a hearty breed. Damn shame if these colonists were outlived by a piece of machinery."

"Bates, they're answering us!"

"Put it on the speakers."

"Repeating. We are unaware of a distress beacon, but we welcome contact with you."

Bates slapped the empty banana peel into the trash slot and smiled. "Well, sir! The beacon's about five hundred years old. But my pappy used to say *better late than never!*"

"Five hundred years? Our planet was bombarded by a tremendous meteor shower five centuries ago. It seems highly unlikely, but perhaps one of our more precocious ancestors had the technology to place such a beacon."

"Yeah, well, give me some landing coordinates and we'll come set a spell. Wait'll you hear how the rest of your ancestors have been getting on!"

The space ship landed.

A huge crowd of Bicanthrans waited, hushed.

Bates walked down the gang plank. She took off her helmet as the Bicanthran president began his speech: "On behalf of all of Biancanthra III, I welcome you -- Oh, my!"

"What kind of puissant damn baby-sitting job is this stupid assignment?!" Captain Angus McFarlane fumed at the mirror. "I'll tell you what kind of puissant damn stupid assignment this is! This is a 'You-only-have-one-year-to-retirement-and-we-don't-want-anymore-incidents-like-Cedarkan-Five' stupid-ass baby-sitting assignment!"

The door buzzed. "WHAT?!"

"The sociologists in charge of the Bicanthra III colonists would like to speak to you, Captain."

"Stupid-ass sociologists," he mumbled under his breath. "By all means, Doctors, do come in."

"I'm Dr. Uri Pansler and this is Dr. Vivian Towers. I understand you've been briefed about the colonists."

"They are a primitive, anachronistic devolvement of our own race. They have been treated as zoo specimens for the last four centuries, and there are only a couple dozen left alive." The Captain ordered coffee for them all. "They are called *Laughing Humans* by the native Bicanthrans, who are quite understandably embarrassed by our arrival."

"And do you know why they're called *Laughing Humans*?" Dr. Towers was as vivacious as her first name seemed to imply. Captain McFarlane, however, was not impressed by vivacious sociologists, even ones with Ph.D.'s in Xenobiology Behavior Modification.

"I have a ship to run, Doctors. We will arrive at Bicanthra III within five solar weeks. After the colonists are on board, we will slowly journey to Datavista VII." The Captain gritted his teeth; the trip could easily be made in less than a month. "In those six months, you two are supposed to help the colonists adapt to our cultural, technological, and social orders."

"I heard you were a real pain!" Pansler smacked his mug down on the obsidian communications table. "Listen. These aren't just aboriginal colonists. They're called Laughing Humans because they don't talk."

"Dr. Munsi Arton -- a native Bicanthran -- you know, Bicanthrans look just like centaurs from out of our old mythology! Anyway, Dr. Arton has always theorized that the colonists choose not to speak. He's fascinating. He's coming with us." Just like most women Angus hated, Dr. Towers turned the conversation away from its crux.

"Anyway," Pansler interrupted. "We did some research. Dr. Arton was right -- the colonists don't permit themselves to speak."

McFarlane got up and paced. "You've got to be kidding."

"No, we checked everything."

"We even have a copy of the colony ship's passenger list; you know how strict 'they' are about genealogy."

"Five hundred years is a long time."

"Captain, they were one of the first Katargan Missionary ships to leave Earth." Towers' hand left a sweaty palm print on the table.8888888888

"Katargan, God!" Pansler shivered. "Makes my skin crawl. I remember stories my mother used to tell to get me to sleep -- kept me awake for hours!"

Angus whistled softly and rubbed his bald head while Towers and Pansler interrupted each other.

"The most powerful --"

"And fanatical --"

"Religion of all time."

"We are going to repatriate the Lost Tribe of Katarga."

Angus whistled louder.

"I wouldn't do that!" Dr. Munsi Arton held the gate shut before Pansler and Towers. "You would terrify them. Outside of their own troop, they have never seen another human -- especially one with clothes."

"We've got to see them!" Pansler whined with excitement.

"Come." Arton led them to the observatory. His four hooves moved rhythmically across the grass while his two hands gestured to many things along the way. "Cameras set up in and around their biostation have given us years and years of tapes. But these view screens over here are live."

Towers was gaping at everything she saw. As they stepped into the artificially cooled observatory, she asked her host, "Dr. Arton, our records show that you have lived with the --"

"Colonists?" Arton smiled.

"The colonists. You've spent years documenting their behaviors."

"I am this planet's authority on the anim-- on the colonists."

He turned on the cameras and focused them.

"This is Bigfeet. She is the leader of the troop."

"Big Feet?"

"I'm sorry, Dr. Pansler. You have to realize we studied them as animals. Speaking with you, I pity and envy the job you have before you."

They watched as Bigfeet walked over to a tall, bearded male. She tapped his left shoulder. The male lay down on his back. Bigfeet straddled him and they rocked ecstatically to an age old rhythm.

"Oh, my." The smooth lining of Arton's triangular-shaped ears turned red. "I never thought of that as anything besides, well -- as animals -- well, my. As you can see, Bigfeet's mate is much younger. We call him Darkarm. He is the youngest male of the troop. He has impregnated Bigfeet ten times. Only three offspring are alive today: the female eating the red-colored root is Beebee; the smaller female up in the tree to the right of the screen is Chichi; and an infant, the one being nursed by the dark-faced female to the left. That female was burned by the barrier; we call her Face. We are not sure of the infant's gender."

They watched quietly as Bigfeet climbed off Darkarm. He stood, shook his shoulders and clapped. Bigfeet smiled and walked away.

"We are hoping Bigfeet is pregnant again. She won't nurse the infant, but she's not had a menstruation since its birth."

"It would be difficult to transport a pregnant," Towers tried not to pause, "colonist. They will have so much to adjust to."

"It will be even more difficult to transport them if Bigfeet does not menstruate."

"Why?" Pansler wiped the slick sheen of sweat from his forehead.

"Haven't you studied the tapes we sent with your probe?"

"Uh, yes, well --"

Towers hated it when her colleague grunted like that. "There were thousands of tapes."

"I see." Arton was offended, but the humans didn't seem to notice the purpling of his ears. "When a female enters menopause and can no longer become pregnant, she is cast out of the troop and quickly dies. If she is the leader, she is sometimes killed by her troop -- by the females only. The males are largely non-aggressive. The troop stays without a leader until a child is born. That infant's mother becomes the new leader."

Arton turned away from the screen to face them. "If you transport them and expect them to sanely accept all that they have to in order to adapt, they will need to have the familiarity of their troop structure."

"How old is Bigfeet?" Towers wondered aloud.

"Do we have to call her 'Big Feet'?" Pansler was ignored.

"About forty-five years. She became leader at the birth of Beebee. Beebee was born two years after the previous leader was cast out. Oh look!" Arton pointed at a female sneaking through the trees. "This is Hunter Rogue. She is my favorite. I know, that's not very objective of me. But she's the last of her species -- note the red pigment of her fur and the scattered melanin pattern in her skin."

"Freckles, we call them freckles." Pansler sneered.

"Oh? Then there are others like her? How delightful!"

"What does she have?" Dr. Towers adjusted the camera's focus.

"A loobuck!" The Bicanthran laughed. "Look! It must outweigh her! That's Hunter Rogue for you."

"How did she kill it?"

"She is the only Laugh-- the only colonist that uses

tools. She uses sharp sticks and rocks mostly, but she hides them in the trees. The others never seem to question how she provides for them."

They watched in awe as Hunter Rogue dragged the loobuck into the clearing. The colonists tore into the buck, their carnivorous instincts coming into full play.

"Remind me to check to colonists for worms," Dr. Towers whispered.

"Mmm, yes, good idea," Pansler replied.

"Actually, I was hoping she would be chosen to mate with Darkarm after Bigfeet is cast out. But then the troop would lose its best food gatherer. Leaders never leave the camp. But if you really want to try to civilize them, I'd start with Hunter Rogue. When I stayed with them, she became almost tame." Dr. Arton didn't observe the uncomfortable looks the human doctors were bestowing on him. "She's most intelligent, even for a human. And she laughs. I've heard her."

Dr. Arton unlocked the gate and led Pansler and Towers inside. The humans looked up, cautious, but not alarmed. They quietly studied the strange female-like creatures, clothed in skin-colored flight suits. The two doctors moved slowly and smoothly into the clearing, with Pansler walking at least two feet behind Towers.

They walked up to Bigfeet and bowed. She did not acknowledge the obeisance, but continued to observe them. Darkarm clutched his baby tightly to his chest.

After five minutes, the doctors sat down. They spent the rest of the day sitting silently in the clearing.

Lying in each other's arms that night, Towers spoke softly, "Did you see Hunter Rogue? She stood watching us the whole time we were with the colonists today."

"Where was she? I counted the other twenty-six, but not her." Pansler brushed his lips across Towers' shoulder.

"She was just inside the barrier. She had something in her hands. It looked like a rope. But it was probably a snake."

"They don't have snakes on this planet," Pansler grunted his 'I know something you don't know' grunt.

"Well, whatever it was didn't move." Towers

huffed.

Pansler blew gently into her ear, apologizing. "You say she just stood and observed?"

After a while, Towers asked, "Did you see the scars on the men?"

"Didn't you hear Munsi's explanation of that?" Pansler grunted again. "When a woman takes a man as mate for the first time, she bites him in the heat of passion. Each bite mark is different. It sort of claims the man and identifies which female he belongs to. The female touches the scar to indicate she wants to --"

Towers rolled on top of Pansler, grinning. "I think it's a great idea. Maybe I ought to bite your shoulder."

"What fun! Then you can slap the wound anytime you feel like having me." He rolled her back over and pinned her arms above their heads.

"Then I'll throw you down on the ground and squat on you." She was much stronger than Pansler and they rolled off the bed and onto the floor.

Pansler gasped and stopped wrestling for a moment. "No wonder they're dying out. How could any human enjoy that five seconds of --"

"Now, Uri, we've been trained to look at behavior environmentally."

"There's nothing environmentally romantic about that."

"That's what you said about the vibrator I bought you last year." Towers ran her hand across his pasty white chest.

"I wonder what they'd think of a vibrator." He snatched her olive-skinned hand to his mouth and kissed her palm.

"Or a food console?" She stood up.

"Or a shower?" He stood with her.

"A bed?" She flung Pansler onto the bed.

"A kiss?" He bent over to kiss her navel.

"What the hell have we gotten ourselves into, Uri?" She patted his back and sighed.

Chapter Two
Hunter Rogue

They spent a week observing each other.

Alarms sounded as Pansler and Towers were eating with the colonists. The colonists headed for the trees and climbed as far up as possible. Pansler and Towers ran with Arton toward the communication viewer at the gate.

"Some animal's got itself caught in the barrier." A guard spoke to Arton. "Procedure says to flush the system, but my supervisor says to check everything through you now," a definite pause, "Sir."

"Meet us at the barrier. Wait for my orders."

The barrier was an electronic tunnel separating two radically different biostations. As the doctors neared it, they found a rope leaning against the barrier, obviously thrown over the top and onto the other side, where it was tied to the branch of a cactus. But somehow, the rope was slipping, dumping slowly

into the barrier a muscular figure. Her arms were full.
She couldn't grab and pull the rope.

"It's Hunter Rogue!" Dr. Arton exclaimed. "She's
used leaves as a basket. And her basket is full of fish!"

The guard commented, "The next biostation is a
desert. Where the hell did it get the fish?"

"Let's worry about getting her out of there first."
Towers suggested.

The guard just stared at her.

"Guard, did you hear Dr. Towers? Find a way to
get the -- colonist out of there." Pansler was out of
breath.

"Great Bitugas -- talking humans!"

"Guard!" Arton growled.

"Yes, sir?" He snapped to attention, but still kept
one eye on Towers.

They hauled on the rope while the guard shut off
the electricity. Hunter Rogue went into convulsions as
her body relaxed from the near deadly voltage.

She hears the New Females talk. The god talks.
The Second New answers him.

And does not die!

The First New speaks to her. Hunter reaches up,
touches the female's lips to feel them move. The

female speaks, and yet the gods do not kill her.

"She doesn't make a sound! She's in agony and doesn't cry out." Towers held Hunter in her arms. Hunter brushed her fingers across Towers' lips. "What kind of taboo would give her that much will power?"

"Katargans believe one only speaks to praise God."

"Katargans?" Arton felt Hunter's pulse.

"It's a long story, Munsi. Let's get Hunter to our ship's sick bay."

"What about her fish?" the guard asked as they walked away.

The smell woke her up. It was wrong. It was like winter -- cold and odorless. But this was not winter. She swam in the lake yesterday.

Memories slowly bounced across her mind: the fire tunnel, fish, much fish, slippery fingers. The fire tunnel snatched her wet feet. The New Females spoke to the gods.

She touched her own lips and sighed. The god had heard her singing to the Sphardiclarkin. He had caught her in his fire tunnel because she sang, and singing was much more like speaking than laughing.

And now she was dead.

She sniffed the air again and opened her eyes.

Gray. Clouds were gray. She was in the clouds. That made sense.

She sat up. Her body hurt. Her feet tingled; the hair was gone from her legs. She nodded knowingly. You must give up something to go to heaven. She had given up her hair.

Still forms snorted in the grayness.

Other dead animals? She hadn't thought about what else might be in heaven. She didn't like dead things. They smelled.

Maybe she would smell, too.

She sniffed again. A change in the wind. It made her head swim. She lay back down and succumbed to the anesthetic.

Uri Pansler typed into the computer:

Day five. We've played subliminal linguistic tapes while the colonists sleep. We sit with them every chance we can.

The colonists are not adapting well to their new environment. Most have refused to eat. Four Fingers has mated repeatedly with Climber; the poor man is exhausted.

Puffy nurses constantly. Some of the older colonists seem catatonic.

This move on board has been much more traumatic than we anticipated.

Dr. Arton suggests we keep them sedated until we bridge the communication gap between us, but our time is limited. In five and a half months, we must arrive with repatriated Katargans, not sedated aborigines.

As Dr. Arton had surmised, the female Hunter Rogue has adapted better than the others. However, she paces the confines of the room constantly. She's discovered the cameras and broken two of them. Dr. Arton cited incidents of similar previous behavior.

We must begin with attempts at verbal communication.

Dr. Towers and I have decided to use basic behavior modification using food.

End of report.

Pansler held up a shiny green disk. He licked it and laughed. He put it in his mouth, took it out and laughed, put it in again and chewed slowly.

Towers picked up a yellow disk. She repeated Uri's procedure, but as she laughed, she said the word "food" softly, as part of the laugh.

Startled, the colonists paid closer attention.

Pansler's laughed "food" was more pronounced.

Bigfeet growled.

Uri and Vivian looked at each other.

Hunter stopped pacing.

Vivian picked around the pile of colored dehydrated disks of food. She picked an orange one up, laughed the word "food" and placed it between Pansler's lips. He laughed "food."

A deep-throated growl preceded Bigfeet. The huge female leaped onto the pile of food disks, glaring at the pair. She flung chips over each shoulder, growling. The pair could not seem to move.

Then Hunter sprang between the doctors and the fierce leader of the troop. She had her back to the doctors, protecting them.

The troop were all on their feet, slapping their chests and thighs, arhythmically.

Hunter slowly squatted on the pile of colors. Her eyes never left Bigfeet's face. Sweat sparkled on her top lip. She took a deep breath and released her bladder.

Hot yellow urine splashed onto the pile of food. The colonists and doctors gasped in surprise.

Bigfeet looked around Hunter at the doctors and curled her lip. She turned back to her mate and sat down, facing ninety degrees away from them. The slapping became clapping as the room rang with laughter.

Hunter turned and leaned towards the astonished scientists. "Food," she said in a whispered laugh.

"Dr. Pansler! Dr. Towers!" The panicked voice woke them. Their new assistant burst into their quarters. "Dr. Towers, Dr. Pansler! I'm sorry, I don't know how it happened. She's gone! The cameras were misaligned!"

"What the hell are you screaming about, Rivers?" Vivian knotted a robe around her.

"The red-headed one -- the -- the colonist!"

"Hunter Rogue?" Uri put his glasses on.

"That's the one. Somehow, the cameras got -- pointed the wrong way. When I found out, I programmed the computer to correct the mistake. I didn't think to count them. There's no way for them to get out!"

"Let me guess, you majored in Literature, right?"

"Sir?"

"Get on with your story!"

"They all woke up when I put their food tray in. They looked around and they all started laughing." Rivers looked at Vivian. "Scariest thing I ever heard."

"And then you counted them." Pansler grunted.

"Yes, sir, and ma'am." Rivers smiled breathlessly at Towers, whose robe hung loose to reveal a wonderful lump of flesh. Pansler grunted again and Rivers cleared his throat before he continued. "Hunter Rogue is missing."

They raced to the observation lab, only to meet Munsi there.

"Now calm down, calm down. She's just up to her old tricks again."

Munsi pointed to Hunter. The female was touching each colonist on the cheek in greeting. Then she lay down on the floor, ignoring the soft pallets against the wall, and went to sleep.

Air comes in. Hunter feels it. This heaven has small nose for breathing. Hunter smells more than winter-cold air. Hunter smells food.

Shiny dead eyes awake at dark. Hunter point eyes at Bigfeet. Lots to see. Hunter pulls cold-stone-web off tunnel, squeeze in, and crawl.

Long, dark, cold tunnel. Then tunnel is bigger. Hunter can sit up and rest.

Light. Hunter crawls toward light. Stone web. Hunter hears water, smells flowers. Air pushes past Hunter into stone web and light.

Next world is all white, but pink shine like shell of Sphardiclarkin. Smooth all around, like inside of egg. Small white flowers on floor. Tall, thinner flowers below her. No sun, but light is there. Like cave of warneal.

Sounds of water.

Animal coming. Cave -- must be cave -- opens and shuts. Animal in baggy skin walks to small flower. Hunter watches. Animal pulls its skin down! It -- she -- sits down. Sounds of water. Female stands and pulls skin back on. Female walks to thin flower and pushes it. Water again. Female washes her hands and stares at side of cave below Hunter. She smiles and pats her cheeks.

Female leaves.

Stone web comes off easy. Hunter drops into cave. Waits and listens. No sounds. She walks to small flower and studies it. Sits on it. Water! Hunter jumps up and studies bowl. Presses lip of blossom. Water shoots up into center of blossom.

Hunter sits back down and enjoys feeling.

Finally, Hunter stands and walks to other flower.

Movement on the wall startles her.

Strange Female stands staring at Hunter. Fierce-looking. Hunter scared.

Hunter show Strange Female signs to go away: Hunter raises and lowers eyebrows. Strange Female stays and raises her eyebrows. Hunter comes step closer and puffs cheeks. Strange Female puffs her cheeks. Hunter curls her lips and shows her strong teeth. Strange Female has very strong white teeth.

Hunter leaps back into air tunnel. Hunter patient. Strange Female will leave. Hunter wants to make water come out of the flowers again.

Noises. Two females. Talking! Hunter covers her face, waiting for god to strike them dead. Then Hunter remembers, *I am dead!* She laughs.

Females stop talking and gasp up at her. Hunter forgot to put stone web back. Female on flower makes horrible noise like baby coming.

Hunter confused. Water in big flower make baby come?

Find out next dark.

Hunter tired. Go home.

Her females laugh as Hunter climbs back out of air tunnel. Hunter pats their faces like other female did. Hunter smiles.

Fun. Good smiles. Everyone happy Hunter goes and comes.

No food this time. Only -- Hunter touches rough, wrinkly faces and remembers smooth soft faces of females in flower room.

Hunter sleeps.

Hunter wakes up and claps her hands. She smiles and walks to small flower in corner of their cave. Must be same flower. Hunter sits and smiles.

"The first sign of civilization is a good toilet."

"Shut up, Uri. This is amazing." Dr. Towers leaned against the lab's one-way mirror, her breath fogging the glass.

"If I may suggest, close off the air vents that might

prove dangerous, but let Hunter Rogue escape as often as she wants." Munsi pawed the floor, proud of his Hunter Rogue.

"I think I'd better clear it through the Captain first." Rivers turned away from the scene below him and sat at the console.

"Nobody asked you, Rivers. Punch up a chart of the ventilation system. Find the ones to close off, and do it."

"Yes, Dr. Pansler."

Chapter Three
Clothing

Uri's report began with a deep sigh:

Day fourteen.

We've noticed a rudimentary sign language, mostly facial expressions, sometimes enhanced by hand and arm motions.

Hunter Rogue has gone into the tunnels every day for a week. She comes back with various items she's taken from the rooms along the ventilation system. Whatever she brings back, she takes immediately to Big Feet. She keeps nothing back for herself.

Most items are accepted by Big Feet -- tasted, and shared.

Some items have been refused by the leader: body powder, a jumpsuit, and -- God knows where Hunter found it -- a flashlight.

Hunter takes the refused items back into the

tunnel. They've been detected by the ship's scanners. Hunter leaves them in a pile three meters in from the colonists' air vent.

Hunter has allowed herself to be seen by the ship's crew. They have been briefed on responsible reactions to our little marauder. We don't believe she presents a danger, but Dr. Arton continues to cite incidences of aggression by captured or cornered females in the past.

The troop -- strike that. The colonists show approval of Hunter's return by the slapping/clapping sounds.

Our nightly, subliminal linguistic lessons have yet to prove fruitful. The Laughing Humans of Bicanthra III still only laugh.

End report.

Good smell! Flowers, mating smell. Good smell.

Hunter watched from an air vent as a naked female sprayed perfume across her breasts, down her thighs, and behind her knees.

Hunter sniffs. Good smell. White Female sat on the edge of the 'bed'. Hunter knows many words now. Bed is for resting.

White Female slowly steps into other skin called

'clothing'. Hunter see many females put on clothing. It still confused her.

White Female picks up small branch and rubs hair with it. She looks at herself in big dead-eye. Other White Female (same-but-dead) looks back. White Female is not frightened by same-but-dead female. She rubs her cheeks and smiles.

Hunter crawls into the room as soon as White Female left. Hunter finds the clear stone with smell inside. She shakes it, presses it, squeezes it. No smell.

Hunter angry. Throws down clear stone on floor. It breaks and smell comes to her.

On hands and knees, she puts her nose into the perfume. It makes her sneeze.

She touches, tastes, spits out the liquid. Then she rubs the perfume all over her breasts, down her stomach to her thighs, and behind her knees.

Hunter stands and faces same-but-dead-Hunter in 'mirror'. It still frightens her a little. The skin underneath the smears of perfume gleams a speckled white. She smiles in mirror.

The small branch smells nice. Hunter rubs her hair with it, but her locks get tangled in the bristles and Hunter finally leaves it hanging from her hair.

She looks 'stupid'. Stupid was new word god tells her last dark.

Hunter goes to cave wall, presses stone, and smiles at her accomplishment as the closet door slides open. Many colors! Grass color is good. Hunter pulls out the green suit and grabs two more as an afterthought.

Hunter must not look stupid. First New wears clothes and looks not stupid.

First New can teach Hunter.

Hunter can teach Bigfeet.

Hunter peeks out of tunnel into her troop's cave. Everyone claps and laughs.

First New is there. She is 'humming'. God is there. He is trying to teach Notoes to wave. They all watch Hunter as she climbs out of tunnel.

Her perfume strikes the troop. They clap and laugh. They rub her breasts and smell her knees.

Darkarm likes smell. Hunter watches Darkarm when Bigfeet isn't looking.

Hunter plops the three outfits in front of Bigfeet, hoping she'll refuse them again.

Hunter holds her breath as Bigfeet touches the

bright grass and sky clothes. Hunter knows Bigfeet likes clothes, but they frighten her, too. They are like dead things.

Bigfeet curls her lip and turns away.

Quickly, Hunter picks up the green and the blue outfits and runs to First New. She thrusts them at her, scared that Bigfeet might stop her.

First New is startled. She looks up questioningly at Hunter.

Hunter sits. Putting her feet into the leggings, she taps First New's legs and then her own.

The troop quiets as they watch.

Hunter pulls the outfit over her legs and taps First New's legs again, this time rubbing the closing seam.

A growl rippled through the expectant hush.

Hunter glares at First New, hoping she will stand up. If she challenges Bigfeet, Hunter could learn so many things. But First New is afraid. Her nostrils flare. She looks from Bigfeet to Hunter and back again.

Hunter crawls across the floor, displaying her full submission to Bigfeet. She holds the blue suit in her hand. When she reaches Bigfeet, she keeps her eyes to the ground and pushes the suit into Bigfeet's lap. She then crawls backwards to First New, keeping her face down.

Hunter takes a deep breath. She was dead, but she was still afraid. Bigfeet did not refuse the outfit. Bigfeet was fingering the material. She watches Hunter closely.

Hunter stands, her back to Bigfeet. First New stands, too.

Hunter slaps her left breast, then pauses. Clamping her lips tightly, Hunter slaps her breasts again, then hits the back of her hand against First New's small breast.

First New is confused, but does not refuse being called Hunter's equal.

Hunter repeats her actions; slapping her breast twice with the palm of her hand, then tapping the back of her hand on First New's breast.

Still no reaction. All Hunter's people begin to stand, uncomfortable with the possibility of an insult.

"Do it, Vivian," Arton whispered. "Do what she did."

Dr. Towers obeyed. She touched her breast and then Hunter's breast. But only once each.

Bigfeet growled again.

Quickly, Hunter signed 'same' again: two-one,

two-one. Dr. Towers understood. She signed 'same'.

The cave rang with clapping, but no laughter.

Hunter sat on the floor and pulled the green outfit onto her legs. First New showed her how to close the material. When she had it on, Hunter walked to each troop member, from the unmated ones first, to the five mated females, and then to Bigfeet.

Bigfeet glared at Hunter, then touched the outfit. She rubbed Hunter's arms and legs, patted her shoulders and back, pulled on the stomach. She sat down, thinking. Then she picked up the blue outfit, handed it to Hunter, and grunted a laugh.

Hunter quickly, nervously put the outfit on her leader. First New came to help close it. Bigfeet allowed everyone (just the females) to touch her sleeve, then clapped.

Hunter dashed back into the tunnel and dragged out enough outfits for everyone. The material adjusted to every body size, even pregnant Tita.

Hunter peeked at Darkarm. He smiled at her. If Bigfeet had seen it, Hunter would be dead now.

His smile seemed to say, "You did something greater than Bigfeet could."

CHAPTER FOUR
Showers

"What died?"

Simple words echoed up to Hunter as she squatted in an air vent. She was exploring new territory. The cave she looked down into was full of 'chairs' and 'tables'. It was a large, dimly lit room. Three cave people sat at one table in the middle.

Garbled words answered the understandable words.

Hunter sniffed the air, not smelling death. She listened carefully to the cave dwellers. They were laughing and putting their hands over their faces. They punched each other playfully and talked about 'bad smell'.

Again, Hunter sniffed and smelled nothing different.

She climbed out of the vent and cautiously approached the three, sniffing, trying to discover what caused their reaction.

They saw her and stopped laughing. She stood still. Maybe one was leader and wanted her submission. She watched their faces for signs of their rank.

They whispered to each other. One reassured the others. It smiled at her and spoke softly.

Hunter smiled back. Encouraged by their calmness, Hunter moved closer, running her hand over the smooth 'tabletop'. She said these words to herself. Gods spoke to her in the dark, telling her the names of things. In light, she touched the items she'd learned and said the words mentally.

One day, she would say the words out loud.

The one smiling pointed to its chest. "Mark." It pointed to her. "Hunterock. Hun-ter-og."

Did it sign 'same'? Hunter came closer, about a table away. She recognized the sound of her name. Mark nodded and repeated its signals.

"Mark. Hunter Rogue."

Hunter slapped her breast. It sounded muffled against the material of the green outfit she still wore.

"Yr Hunter Rogue." The cave dweller tapped its chest and smiled. "Im Mark."

Hunter, Mark -- same! Hunter was surprised. She smiled and leaped onto the chair next to her new friend.

"Dear God!" The cave people at the table covered their faces and made strange noises. They puffed out their cheeks.

Hunter was scared. She jumped away from them. Mark was making sounds of anger.

Hunter signed 'same', but as she bent to slap Mark's chest, it jerked away from her.

Hunter slowly crept back up to her air vent.

She returned to her troop empty-handed and angry.

First New was there. Hunter bowed to Bigfeet and then walked over and sat down next to her friend.

First New touched her hair and hummed, "Hunter?" Hunter grabbed First New's hand and held it to her nose. She sniffed.

First New had no scent.

Hunter sniffed up First New's arm to her armpit and neck. Her hair smelled like trees in summer. Nothing else about First New smelled. Hunter pried her mouth open and smelled. Even her breath was nice.

"Same," Hunter signed. "Same," she repeated, hitting hard.

"Same," Vivian signed gently.

Hunter curled her lips and puffed her cheeks. She took First New's hand and pressed it against her nose. Then she pressed her own hand against First New's nose.

Vivian gagged, like the people in the table-chair cave.

Hunter stood up and walked away, deeply hurt.

Vivian jumped up, then hesitated. She clapped her hands and took a deep breath. Slowly, she took off her outfit.

The troop watched in habitual silence.

Her skin was dark, hairless. She walked to the flower and sat on it. The water swooshed. She stood up and walked into a niche in the wall. She touched the wall. Rain fell only on her.

She smiled and laughed. She exaggerated the motions of taking a shower.

Hunter already had her suit off. She began pressing the walls, asking the cave to give her rain, too.

First New took her hand and let her stand under the rain. Warm rain! Like summer. First New rubbed something on her skin that smelled like trees. The dark layers of dirt smeared and ran down her legs. The skin underneath was pale and freckled. It was the most wonderful feeling Hunter ever remembered.

The tree smell overwhelmed her own scent. Her skin changed colors from rusty brown to shell pink. The itches in her hair stopped. Hunter let First New bathe her and didn't care that the whole troop was watching.

Mark would not hold its nose now.

Plenty of times, Hunter's scent had saved her life. Most carnivores eat good-smelling animals, not strong musky animals like her. But that time was gone.

It was time to live like these cave dwellers.

While the other females showered, Vivian brought combs and brushes in and showed Hunter how to use them. Hunter recognized the small branch. Now she would learn to use it right.

Vivian's hair was short, but the colonists were tenderly impatient with their long hair. Vivian left the cave and returned with something covered. She went to Hunter first.

"Same?"

"Same," Hunter assured her happily.

First New lifted Hunter's hair, then ran her fingers

through her own short curls. "Same?"

"Same." Hunter would learn whatever First New wanted to teach her. She sat patiently as First New put a cold thing to her hair. Her hair fell into her lap.

Bigfeet was too busy enjoying her shower to notice.

Hunter's rust-colored locks fell in a matted heap onto her lap. She caught Darkarm's eyes again. He smiled admiringly, aware that Bigfeet could not see him.

Then Vivian picked up the fallen hair, covered the scissors, and left the room. Dr. Arton begged for Hunter's first hair clippings. They are still his favorite possession.

Vivian ordered new outfits for every female. The five males still refused to dress or wash.

Dr. Rivers whispered, "Can you teach me how to bathe tonight?" for which he received a bruise.

A few other females wanted their hair cut. But for the most, the shower was quite enough adaptation at one time.

Hunter showered every evening before her excursions into the air vents. She took off her outfit and went naked in her own cave, but always put on a clean outfit after her shower before going into the vents.

She was unsure of herself now, aware of the way the cave people looked at her. She tried to find Mark in the table-chair cave, but couldn't. Whenever she got to a cave, she couldn't bring herself to go through.

After a week of failed courage, Hunter decided to return to the first cave she'd discovered. She waited, sweating with fear and cowardice. Pushing gently against the 'screen', Hunter slipped into the 'bathroom' and breathed deeply the flower scented air.

She touched the 'toilet', she turned on and off the 'sink.' She looked up at the 'mirror'. A different Hunter stared back than the one she remembered from weeks ago.

As she stared, amazed and pleased, a cave female came in. The female smiled and went about her business, not paying Hunter any mind.

The cave female said something to Hunter as she washed her hands. It wasn't a question, it was a friendly statement. Hunter smiled gently. The cave female smiled back. It was a warm, equal smile.

The cave female turned and walked to the wall.

The wall opened, the female walked through, the wall closed again.

Hunter took a deep breath and walked through the 'door' into a new world.

Chapter Five
Stars

Hunter had been roaming the vast hallways of the 'cave' for weeks when she made the most amazing discovery: some of the cave people were males!

She had always assumed the cave people were all female. Males -- well, they were just for mating. The outfits covered the genitalia and Hunter had never questioned it.

Hunter walked into a bathroom with another cave person. It looked at her with a strange expression, but then shrugged and opened its outfit. Hunter was so surprised she repeated a phrase she'd heard before. She actually said it out loud, "Dear God!"

The cave male said something he thought was funny and closed one eye. Hunter ran out of the cave.

She found a 'long chair' in a hallway and sat down. She carefully studied the people who passed her and began to distinguish subtle differences that might indicate gender, but she noticed no deference shown by one to another.

The 'males' were sometimes bigger in the shoulders, smaller in the hips. The 'females' had very small breasts, but Hunter noticed some size variations. The females' faces were thinner and sometimes had colors painted on. The males' faces were more square and although some she thought might be male had colors on their faces, she was too confused to decide what they were.

Her people-- you just looked and knew. Why would the cave people hide what they were?

Hunter must learn why. How did they tell the difference?

She smiled at what she thought was a female. It smiled back. She smiled at a possible male. It smiled back. That wasn't the answer.

Hunter remembered the strange facial expression of the male in the bathroom. She shut one eye and looked at a possible male. It copied her expression. She tried again at a female. It scowled at her!

Hunter sat for an hour, winking and observing the reactions between males and females. Most of the ones she thought were male winked back, most of the ones she thought were female scowled or ignored her; but some females winked back, smiling, and some males ignored her.

There must be another way to tell the difference. Hunter sat for another hour, observing their walk, their speech, their mannerisms. There was very little difference. Then Hunter realized something -- she had never seen a cave female mate. She wondered if they did.

First New would know. Trying to explain her question to First New would be hard.

An opportunity to learn came the next day. Both First New and Second New came into the troop's cave together. Hunter jumped up and ran to First New.

"Same," was greeted by "same." Looking closely, she noticed Second New had a thin but square face. Its shoulders were larger than its hips. It had no visible breasts. Cautiously, Hunter faced Second New. She watched First New's reaction as she slowly reached out and touched Second New's left shoulder.

The doctors had already discussed this possibility. Vivian growled softly and Hunter snatched her hand back, faced the floor, and walked away.

Hunter kept to herself inside her cave the rest of that day. She was confused by her discoveries. She was unmated, and yet was greeted as an equal by First New. In her troop, (and so, in her heart) she was not equal to a mated female. She'd never seen her friend mate Second New. Could it be that cave people covered themselves because they don't mate?

Hunter would find out.

For two days, Hunter explored the air vents, using her sense of smell to search for First New's cave.

She'd almost given up when she heard a soft laugh and a familiar voice. She followed the sounds and worked herself into the air vent leading into Pansler's and Towers' room. Hunter could not see them. She smelled food. She heard them talking, every now and then she caught a word she recognized.

She waited, pressed against the vent, straining to see First New and her mate. The 'door' opened as Second New came into the room. Hunter watched him undress. His back was smooth and hairless, not at all like Darkarm -- whose back was covered by thick brown fur. Second New touched the light off before he crawled into bed. The door opened again as First New walked in. She undressed in the dark. Hunter heard her crawl under the 'bed clothes'. The people murmured to each other.

Hunter woke up to find herself wedged against a screen. She stretched and looked around. First New and her mate were pressed against each other, but light was coming from the top of the cave. Hunter's knee joint popped and Second New turned over.

Hunter squinted at his left shoulder. "Dear God!" she whispered.

Second New had no scar.

"I don't know what's up with Hunter Rogue lately." Dr. Rivers drummed his fingers on the table.

"What do you mean?" Pansler was eating a jelly sandwich.

"She's been hauling in more junk than a flea marketer on Saturday." Rivers pointed to the view screen. "Look at that! Every day, she's brought in pretty baubles and food and given it all to Bigfeet."

"Yeah, some of the crewmen are beginning to complain," Towers agreed.

"It's almost like she's bribing Bigfeet." Rivers stopped drumming.

"That's exactly what she's doing, but I don't understand why." Munsi scratched his left ear. "The only favor Bigfeet could bestow is a mate, but there are no available males."

"Maybe she knows something we don't. Like one of the mated females might be sick or something." Towers studied the view screen.

"Maybe she met someone on the other side of her air vents and is planning on bringing him home to meet Mama," Rivers wiggled his eyebrows at Uri.

"Don't be gross!" Pansler sneered.

"But you are the same species."

The two men glared at the Bicanthran while Vivian laughed.

"Whatever she's up to, it's going to be good." Vivian typed up a graph on the computer. "Look. We've completed our intelligence tests on the colonists. Bigfeet, her three children, Roundjaw, Notoes, Scarleg, and Fang all have average to low average quotients. The others range from average to above average. But look at these two --"

Rivers read, "Hunter Rogue and Darkarm."

Pansler gasped, "Those are higher than m-- yours!"

"Damn right!"

"And look at their learning modalities. Darkarm is a strong diverger-accommodator. Hunter is a strong assimilator-converger."

"If we could only mate them, what a fine breed we could -- oh, my."

"That's all right, Munsi." Vivian innocently patted his head. "Actually, I was thinking along the same lines."

Uncomfortable looks passed between Rivers and Pansler.

The Bicanthran patted Vivian's bottom -- fair exchange for her seductively patting his head. "Well, we'll just keep an eye on things and hope something happens soon."

"Before the Captain gets wind of Hunter Rogue and her scavenging." Rivers turned back to the viewer.

"I wonder why he's never come down here," Pansler mused.

"I've never met the human, but your library has a fascinating bio on him." Munsi adjusted a camera Hunter Rogue had messed with.

"Well, I've met him," Rivers put his hands on his

hips. "And I hope he never comes down here!"

"Why, Rivers, you sound scared of the man," Pansler sneered.

Rivers gaped and gulped and nodded at him. "You're right. The stories I've heard! Even the Cedarkan V episode was enough to . . . Well, he's got this walk."

"His walk?" Vivian laughed.

'The way he walks. It's --" Rivers blushed and fidgeted with his control panel. "It's like he's saying 'I am master of all I survey and you are but dust beneath my feet!'"

Finally, the day came for Hunter to put her plan into effect. First New walked in, greeted Bigfeet, then began examining the children. Second New walked in and greeted Bigfeet, who ignored him completely since she still thought of him as an inferior female.

Hunter sprang on Second New, threw him to the floor and ripped open his suit, exposing his left shoulder. Easily pinning him with her legs, Hunter clapped and clapped. First New stood above her, growling. Hunter only curled her lips in contempt.

Bigfeet touched her arm, Hunter got off of the male. He stood, scared of the large females around him. Bigfeet pressed her lips together, careful not to show First New any teeth. She brushed back the male's clothes and looked at his virgin shoulder.

Bigfeet smiled. The others laughed and clapped. Bigfeet scanned the unmated females, calculating the benefits of any possible matings. She knew who she would choose, but she had to meet each gaze. She paused while looking at First New. The cave female had protected the male once, and yet had claimed equality with Hunter; the two must be siblings.

Bigfeet looked at Hunter. She was naked and sweaty. Bigfeet remembered when she had felt the same way. It was Hunter's mother who had given her Darkarm.

It was such a scrawny male, though. Bigfeet wished she could find a large, strong, furry male for Hunter.

But she was taking too long and Hunter was getting frightened. Bigfeet smiled, took Hunter's hand, and placed it on Second New's left shoulder. The troop laughed and clapped.

Hunter slowly removed her male's clothing. He wasn't very exciting to look at -- no hair, slick pale skin. But he was her chance to be mated.

First New growled and whined. She sounded terribly frightened. Hunter ignored her, knowing the others would tolerate no interruption.

Hunter put her hand on the male's shoulder and pushed him to the floor. She sat on his thighs and waited. Nothing happened.

She gingerly probed the male with her fingers. His skin was as smooth as the table top. She rubbed her palms across his stomach, marveling at the sensations. Her friends were crowded around, curious.

Hunter could see Darkarm out of the corner of her eye. He looked angry as he held his baby.

Still nothing happened. Hunter looked up at Bigfeet. Her leader smiled and motioned at Darkarm. He laid down beside Second New. Bigfeet demonstrated everything Hunter could touch and do to make mating possible. Hunter repeated everything she saw and was surprised by her affects.

Then Bigfeet and Darkarm got up. Hunter got onto her knees and pressed herself down onto Second New. The pain was horrible! Flesh ripped and tore, yet a rhythm took over and she ripped herself again and again against his hard flesh. When the pain was almost too much and she was afraid she would cry out, Hunter leaned over and sank her teeth into her mate's left shoulder. His fingers clawed into her back. It was the first time he had touched her. His whole body shuddered.

Hunter rose, the taste of his blood in her mouth. Bigfeet embraced her. The other mated females embraced her, sharing her silent pain. But Hunter didn't know it had hurt them, too, the first time. She thought Second New had done it on purpose. No wonder these cave people covered themselves if it hurt so much to mate.

Hunter stayed in the cave for the next few days. She didn't care that Second New left and hadn't returned. She hoped he never came back again.

She found herself staring at Darkarm more and more. She would never know if he hurt or not. Her caught her watching him a few times and turned sadly away.

A mated female did not have to hunt, but after a week of boredom, Hunter disappeared into the tunnels one night and returned smiling. She went out again, night after night, and discovered more ways to become like the cave people.

They very rarely noticed she was different now. She walked like they did, she dressed like they did, she even began speaking to them.

One night, she found her way into a cafeteria. The smell of food attracted her, and her looks attracted a male sitting there. He smiled and gestured for her to join him.

Hunter looked hungrily at the dark brown heap on the male's plate.

"Wojalixomkak?"

Hunter nodded. "Food."

"Ine food, or wojalixomkak?"

"Wojali-kak." She pointed at his plate.

"Cake." The man laughed. He pressed the table and said it again, "Cake."

The center of the table opened, pushing up another slice of dark chocolate cake. Hunter looked at the male, then reached for the new taste.

She nibbled a piece, the gobbled it up. "Good. Damn good wojali-cake."

The male laughed. "Wojali more cake?"

Hunter paused. The male was too happy about her eating. He had not finished his own cake. She did not want to be stupid.

"No." She licked her lips, proud of her restraint.

The male pressed the table and said, "To kofes."

The center delivered them. He handed her a cup and smiled. She observed him blow the steam, sip, blow again, sip, put the cup down. She mirrored his actions.

"Yr pritequt. Minams Sam."

Hunter recognized the gesture. Cave dwellers were not 'same', so they just pointed to themselves.

"Un-tar," she smiled.

"Reyalqut. Unu-onbord?"

"Yes. Damn good cake."

"R-u-hungre?" His expression was different than she had seen before.

"Un-tar, no Un-gre."

"Ha, ha. Thaspri-te Damn qut!" He put his hand on her arm.

"Qut?" She didn't remember the word in her nightly conversations with god.

"Shur, qut." He rubbed his hand up to her elbow. "Wojalikta go?"

"Go good?" She hoped 'go' was more food.

"I 'go' damn good!" He took her hand and led her out of the cafeteria. They walked side by side, he still had her hand. Soon, they reached another door which opened into the noisiest confusion Hunter had ever seen. She pulled away, scared.

"Izalri Darlin. I li-ta danz a lil for we 'go good'." He pulled her into the dark cave. Lightening flashed across the ceiling, thunder boomed against her eardrums.

Hunter found herself held tightly in Sam's arms, pressed against him in the most uncomfortable way. The room was packed with other cave people. Hunter was so terribly frightened, she couldn't move on her own.

Sam rubbed her back and squeezed her bottom. Then he pressed his mouth onto hers and stuck his tongue between her teeth.

Hunter decided that cake and coffee taste good only when you are the one who ate them.

Hunter's flight-instinct took control and she pushed her way through the crowd. She ran out an exit and kept running. She ran until the halls were empty of people and the lights of 'day' began to brighten in the ceilings. Exhausted, her adrenaline level back to normal, Hunter chose a doorway and slipped quietly inside.

The room was narrow and long. One 'long chair' ran down the left side of the room. She sank next to it and put her head down on the seat.

She was sound asleep when a finger pressed against the pulse in her wrist. She woke to the sound of a gentle voice. "R-u-o-k?"

Hunter looked up into a wrinkled, hairless face. It did not smile at her. She could tell instinctively it was a leader and she needed to show submission. She dropped her eyes and sat up.

The hairless leader turned its back on her and grumbled something at her. It walked to the expanse of the wall opposite the long chair and pressed it. The wall faded away and bright balls of distant fires swirled in a stasis grand.

"Dear God!" Hunter breathed.

The leader glared at her, then became captivated by her look of total innocence. He held out his hand to her -- for now she noticed his build. She walked to him, equally amazed by the panorama as she was by a dominant male.

She took his hand and stood by his side. He was impressed by her silence. So often, women tried to tell him what they were seeing and how it made them feel.

This woman explained all that in her expression and silent awe. His skin tingled. Her warm hand pressed firmly into his.

Captain McFarlane believed that true camaraderie struck instantly and lasted a life time. As he stood beside this woman, he felt his spirit bind itself to her.

Hunter looked up at him once, deep into his ice blue eyes. They seemed as deep and powerful as what she saw before them.

"Stars?"

The word whispered in the room lit the old man's heart. "Stars," he replied.

Chapter Six

Angus

Hunter followed the Hairless Male Leader down a long, bright hallway. He spoke softly in such a way that Hunter didn't need to respond verbally. She was attentive with her eyes and her expression. Even though she didn't understand all his words, his tone told her to pay attention and be respectful.

They stopped outside a door. The Hairless Male Leader looked deeply into her eyes again. She felt both lost and found.

"Itslat. Wojalixom coffee?"

"Coffee. Cake." Hunter felt honored and smiled at the floor.

He touched her chin, pulling her eyes up to meet his. "Donluk down. U havesuch wizdom enyr iz."

A cave male turned into their hallway. The Leader dropped his hand. He quickly led her into a large room.

Deep rich, earthy colors touched the cave. The long chair was squishy- looking. The walls were lined with 'shelves'. Objects of different shapes and sizes rested on the shelves. A lope skull stood upright on a shiny stick. A round ball with browns and greens spun by itself; nothing held it up or kept it going.

Hunter moved cautiously to the shelves. She desperately wanted to touch the things and talk about them. So many new things!

"Two coffees -- blak. Dju tak inetheng enyr coffee?"

"Cake." Hunter turned quickly. She was almost afraid the shelves might disappear before she could turn back to them.

"Coffee-cake, one sliz." The food console quietly opened to reveal his order. He left it there and joined her. She reached for a small box, but nervously pulled her hand back. He was a leader. It was not right to touch without permission.

"Here. This izamuzik box." He picked it up, opened it, and the tinkling melody began.

Hunter held it gently and studied it with a little fear. "Bird. Box."

"I donges yuv evr cenna muzik box. This izan old one."

"Old?" Hunter rubbed the inlaid woods, believing that they might have grown that way. "Old bird?"

"It duzound lika bird, duznit?" He placed it back on the shelf.

"Lope." Hunter pointed at the skull she recognized.

"Yes. Mifathur shotit. Bak wen men didsuch thengs." He was pleased by her look of admiration.

"This iza repracentashun uvmiwerld, Earth. It wuzmad bithu Mumgosi."

Hunter couldn't understand his garbled words, but she felt no threat. She touched the surface of the spinning ball and pulled back wet fingers.

"This?!" She pointed at the globe, careful not to touch it again.

His eyes twinkled, "Thu Mumgosi exselin akurase."

His syllables raced past her ears, indistinguishable, so she returned to words she recognized. "Earth home?"

"Yes, wunz." His voice was sad.

"Hurt?"

"Yes. Sumemores du hurt."

"Sumemores dead," she thought she understood.

"No, memores dondie."

Hunter was afraid she had saddened her new friend. She looked around, trying to cheer him up.

'Glass. Stone. Fire. Small tree." Hunter pointed at objects and shyly identified them. "Fish in water. Bone. Hunter!" She stopped in front of a recessed mirror set between the shelves.

The Hairless Male Leader placed his hands on her shoulders and peered into the mirror, too. "Shal Untar beapart uvmi kulekshun, two?"

He wanted her to do something. His eyes were sad, but his hands were firm. She trembled, wanting so much to say the right thing. Her vocabulary failed her. She shrugged, rubbing her cheek against his hand.

He felt her distress. "Kum havyr coffee."

They sat on the long chair and sipped peacefully.

He spoke softly for a while, pointing at different things and telling her about them. She listened, trying to absorb every syllable.

Time passed, and they ordered more coffee, and

he told her all about his life. She listened with a naive grace and emotional perception.

She was so unlike the women he knew. They all wanted to comment on similarities, argue on differences, change to an unrelated subject. She was the first woman who ever truly listened to him. Her expressions deeply touched him. He longed to touch her hair, brush his fingertips across her thighs. He was mesmerized by her bright green eyes.

He hadn't felt this way in years.

A beep startled Hunter. The Hairless Male Leader scowled and touched the table in front of them. The table said something; the male grumbled a reply and then turned to face her. She was upset. Had there really been someone inside the table?

The captain took her hands and pressed them to his lips. "I must go."

She was moved by this new gesture. "Go -- hurt?"

"Untar," the man stood up, pulling her to her feet. "Watferme. Itmitbe afu ors, but don go. Plez."

"Hunter don go."

"Delitful woman!" He pulled her into his arms and pressed his lips into her hair two or three times. He smelled good. His arms were strong.

As strange as it seemed to her, Hunter didn't want him to let go.

After he left, Hunter touched every item on the shelves. She studied the strange logs that opened, filled with leaf-like things. She thought about eating a fish, but didn't want to offend the Hairless Male Leader. She was fascinated by his things, but she couldn't put names to them and that irritated her. Why hadn't the gods told her about such things? Wasn't she worthy enough? They told her about chairs and toilets, soap, smell, clean, numbers, up, down. . .

She looked into the mirror again and shivered. She wanted to feel the male's hands on her shoulders again. But then what? She was so confused.

Hunter examined the entire room and then went into the bedroom. She mentally categorized that room as well: things she could identify, things she would ask him about.

He had a 'smell glass', too. It smelled just like him.

She yawned. She got undressed and took a shower. She had been so respectful, but before she crawled into bed, she couldn't resist. She sprayed his scent between her breasts.

The sheets were warm. The room darkened

automatically -- the computer sensed her presence on the bed. Hunter fell into a deep, peaceful sleep.

"Stupid-ass old fool!" Angus McFarlane cursed himself for being disappointed when he found his living room empty.

He walked dejectedly into his darkened bedroom, undressed and crawled under the covers. When he found her next to him, he laughed out loud.

Hunter woke, frightened by her strange surroundings, but then a familiar smell and voice calmed her.

The male was touching her face.

"I thot --" he pulled her hair away from her cheeks. "I thot ilost u."

His words were so full of emotion, Hunter trembled. She would probably die for touching this leader, but he really didn't seem to mind. Her fingertips brushed his left shoulder, where on his outfit had sparkled five shiny stones. Her astonishment showed on her face. No scar! He had no mate! Could it be that someone so old and so -- wonderful was not mated?

"Imnot thukapten here. En this bed, Im Angus." He pulled her against his chest and whispered in her ear. "Dyu herme, Untar? Angus."

He pressed his lips against her hair again, on her cheeks, against her eyes. It felt wonderful, but this was so new. Hunter wanted to do this right and not seem stupid to Angus. She repeated his actions. Wherever he pressed his lips, she pressed hers. Wherever he caressed her body, her fingers discovered the same places on his body.

This was the most exciting learning she'd ever done. She knew muscles and flesh and blood, but it never occurred to her that tickling and pressing and sucking and licking and holding -- Well, she had just never thought of it that way before.

His lips pressed against her cheek, she pressed hers against his and wound up lips to lips. He nibbled her lips, all around first, and then opened his mouth. Hunter remembered Sam in the lightening-thunder cave. Was this what he was trying to do? It felt so different.

Hunter gingerly licked her tongue between his teeth, and then pulled back. He shuddered and rolled on top of her.

She couldn't breathe. She was trying to learn all this, but she couldn't think! She was still mirroring his actions, so when he rubbed her belly, she slid her hands down his chest.

What she found below his navel frightened her. "No!" She tried to get out from under him. He had her firmly pinned to the mattress. "No! Hurt Hunter! Angus hurt Hunter!"

"I wont hurt you. Untar!" He cupped her face in his gentle hands. "Untar, Untar, plez. Wont hurt you." His lips drank up the tears they found on her face. He slowed down, trying to control his passion.

"Mate hurt Hunter," she whispered, trying to explain.

"Bastard, Ottobe kastrated."

She peered into his eyes, trying to understand his anger.

"Angus?" She was so scared and so confused.

"Yes?" He pulled away from her.

Her vocabulary was too damn limited. She must get him to understand. She ran her hands across his curly chest, exciting the nipples he'd taught her to kiss. She patted her breast, tapped his chest. If he was going to kill her for this impudence, at least she'd enjoyed the last days of her life.

"Same. Hunter, Angus, same."

"Yrso damn purseptive, Untar. Yes, werthu same. Yr mate hurt you; mi mate hurt me." He rubbed her hand against his chest. "I nevr thot id luvagin. But I fellenluv withu thuminit you tukmihand. Iswar, I wilnevr hurt you, Untar. And you wilnevr hurt me."

Then the most amazing thing happened. It didn't hurt. He pulled her under him, pressed himself against her, and like a cave door, she seemed to open to him and take him in. It felt like swimming in a warm pool, and a little like getting caught in the fire tunnel. Her breath came in gasps, so did his. Her arms and legs rippled and shuddered, as if they had a life of their own.

There was no cave, no people, no gods; only her and Angus and the stars.

"I don't know where she is!" Dr. Pansler yelled. "Not even the ship's computer can track her. She's human! How the devil do you expect the computer to pick out one human from eight hundred humans?"

"She's been gone three days and I really think we ought to notify the captain."

"Rivers," snapped Pansler. "Someone ought to notify your brain that it's stuck up your -"

"What, an anatomy lesson from the likes of you?" Rivers put his hands on his cheeks. "Oh, my!"

"You know what's going to happen to us if -- if anything!" Pansler jabbed another graph onto the computer. "We'll be lucky if they let us observe streptococci bacilli in a petri dish!"

"I told you when she first got out --"

"Go abstain, Rivers!"

"Well, if you can't be a good hubby and keep the little wifey-po at home." Rivers ducked as Uri's fist dented a control panel close to River's head.

"This is fascinating!" Dr. Arton was making quick sketches, taking it all in. "I hadn't realized how aggressive human males could become! You totally revert to the primitive instincts of your females when threatened."

They froze, gaping at the Bicanthran.

"Please don't stop, this is astonishing!"

Chapter Seven
God and gods

She wore his 'robe' and held the 'music box' in her hand. She hummed the now familiar tune. He sat by her side 'reading' from a 'book'.

She'd been with him five darks and her vocabulary was growing by leaps and bounds.

"Angus, like music?"

"Yes, I'm especially fond of the harp."

"Harp good?"

"Harp is the best."

"Hunter-I hear harp?"

"Sure." Angus pressed several 'buttons' on the table and a rich sound filled the air. Hunter listened attentively. She picked out the melody and sang. She sang only vowel sounds, sometimes losing her strain, but never her pitch.

"What a beautiful voice!" Angus put down the book. "You amaze me. I didn't know you could sing."

"Sing. Hunter-I make music sing."

"Sing only for me."

"No, I sing for things.   Have you."

"What?" He adored her accent. It was a challenge to understand her. With all the Alliance's technical advances, they had never developed a universal language. Most people spoke a pigeon of Alliance; their accents made life more exciting.

"I sing for fish."

"I hope the fish appreciate it."

"Fish dead."

"You sing for dead fish?"

"Yes. Eat fish."

"You sing to get fish to eat!"

"Yes," Hunter patted Angus' leg in praise. "Angus smart. Good."

"I'm damn smart!"

"You damn good, too!" She rubbed his leg and smiled.

"Who gives you the fish? To whom do you sing?"

"Spardiclarkin like Hunter sing. Sphardiclarkin," she paused and signed 'give', "fish for Hunter sing."

"What the hell are Sphardiclarkins?"

Hunter thought, taxing her language. She rubbed her tongue across her teeth, thinking.

"Much big." She rubbed her chest and pointed to her teeth. "Hard, smooth out." She opened her mouth and pointed at the soft underside of her tongue. "In."

"What planet are they from?"

"Water. Deep warm water."

"No, Untar. Planet, like Earth. What is the name of their planet?"

"Zoo." She'd heard that word before from a caveman that recognized her.

"I hate zoos. I can't stand to watch those poor animals caged up. I'd rather be dead than live in a zoo!"

His words shocked her. She understood 'zoo', 'animals', 'dead', 'hate', and his tone of disgust.

"Angus, Hunter; same. Hunter, animal; same. Angus, animal; no same?"

"Stupid-ass scientists say we are. But I'll tell you, Untar -- you and I are not animals. We saw the stars and have tried to conquer them. Animals see the stars, but they can't understand them. Can't feel their power, nor hear their call."

"Not animals? Not gods."

"No, we're not God. I think we're stuck

somewhere in-between."

"Angus know gods?"

"Yes. I was raised by a strong Christian woman. Went to church every Sunday and most Wednesdays, too. I guess I sort of lost Him along the way, but I believe I'll meet up with Him again, soon enough."

Thinking he meant that he'd run away from the gods, she asked, "Gods scare Angus?"

"No, why should He?" He found she had curled her knees under her chin and was whispering. "Untar, you shouldn't be afraid of God."

"Gods eat babies."

"He does not!"

"Gods eat old ones, yes."

"Not my God!"

"Gods ugly!" She leaned toward him and whispered fiercely, "Untar hate gods!"

She knew he was angry with her for saying it, but she had felt that way all her life. He gritted his teeth in silence. She got up and put the music box back. Still he would not speak.

The harp music stopped. Angus pretended to read, but Hunter could tell he was still angry.

She dropped to the floor and rested her

forehead on his knees. Still he did not speak. She began to tremble. "Hunter go?"

He slipped his hand through her hair, caressed the back of her head, pulled her up to face him. "Hear me good. Angus die if Untar go."

She threw herself around him and cried. He cried, too.

They were visiting the 'observation deck' again. The stars wandered across the screen. Blues and greens, giants and dwarves: hints of the enormity of time. It was Hunter's favorite of all places except for Angus' bed.

"Angus?" They were usually silent during their visits here, but Hunter had been thinking and she needed to understand this concept of 'God' as opposed to 'gods'. "Tell me of God of Angus."

The gentle power of his voice thrilled her: "'Oh Lord, our Lord! How majestic is Your name in all the Earth! When I see the heavens, the works of Your fingers, the moon and the stars which You have formed; what is man that You should think of him, the son of man that You should care for him? Yet You've made him but little lower than God, and crown him with glory and honor! You make him ruler over the works of Your hands, You have put all things under his feet: all sheep and oxen, and also the beasts of the field, the birds of the heavens and the fish of the sea that travel the paths of the ocean.' Psalm Eight, or there about."

Hunter was silent for a moment while he massaged her shoulders and breathed gently into her hair. She kissed the back of his hand, then whispered, "Good words. New -- new see. Tell more."

"My Sunday school teacher would be proud of me. She would have adored you -- your innocence. She wanted me to go into the ministry. It just about broke her heart when I was accepted into the Alliance Academy. It was partially her training that prepared me. She made me memorize one passage a week. That was years ago -- no, decades ago."

She smiled at him with that all-knowing, empathetic smile he had sought after all his life.

He turned her away from the stars to face him. "Dya know the Bible, Untar?"

"No. Angus' God words -- Bible?"

"Yes. The Bible is the word of God."

She thought for a while.

"Angus? Angus God and Hunter god not same. Angus God good. Hunter god not good. Not -- not 'god'."

He traced the line of her jaw and studied the deep places of her eyes. "There are a lot of religions floating about; I'm Christian. You're probably right; our gods may not be the same."

"I must know. Go. Come back. Must find god, see if -- see who god, who animal, see who Hunter."

He smiled bravely, hoping that she really would come back to him, but a fire-hot poker jabbed his chest. He had let her mean too much to him. She kissed him, turned away, and left.

When she was sure he was not following her, she stopped a caveman. "I'm lost. Find zoo."

"Sue? I don't know any Sue." The caveman walked away.

She tried again with the next passerby. "I'm lost. Must find Zoo. Zoo not good word. Help, please."

"Use the computer." The caveman pointed to the wall and walked off.

Hunter walked over and examined the pulsing 'buttons'. She touched one. "Zoo."

"Specify, please."

"Find Zoo."

"Library catalogue on 'zoo' is extensive. Please specify."

"Planet." Hunter began to sweat. "Planet Zoo."

"Unable to locate information as requested." The lights softened and the voice stopped.

"Damn stupid!" Hunter hit the wall with her fist.

"Name, please."

"Hunter."

"Christian or appellate?"

She remembered hearing Angus use one of those words. She repeated it. "Christian."

"Appellate, please."

"Tell again."

Last name and/or rank."

"Hunter Rogue."

"One moment."

Kilometers away, Rivers' communications set flashed. "You're not gonna believe this-" He typed commands into his keyboard and pressed 'enter'. "Let's go! I'll explain on the way!"

"Hunter Rogue. Stay. Wait." The voice from the wall spoke again.

"Hunter lost. Must find Zoo."

"Hunter Rogue. Stay. Wait."

"Damn stupid -- 'stay, wait'. Go find. Must find!"

"Hunter Rogue. Stay. Wait."

She was waiting by the computer as Rivers, Towers, and Pansler ran down the hallway. They stopped, steadied each other, and walked slowly towards her.

First New began humming softly. It made Hunter angry. "Talk good. Gods not eat."

"She can talk!"

"Great observation, Pansler. How the hell dya think the comp-"

"Just once, would the two of you stop squabbling! We need to be calm, not frighten Hunter Rogue." Towers held up her hand.

"Stupid-ass not scare Hunter-I."

"My God!"

"Hunter-I not god. Not animal. Hunter Rogue is --" this concept was still vague to her. "Hunter no animal. Must find zoo. Talk to god-no-god."

"Are you recording this?" Rivers hissed.

"Zoo? It's not a zoo, Hunter." Vivian spoke softly.

"Animal -- zoo."

"Hunter hungry? Much food at zoo. We take Hunter home."

"Shut up, Pansler. She's not an idiot!"

Rivers smiled with delight as Towers snapped at his rival.

"Pansler?" Hunter pointed at Second New.

"Yes. My name is Uri Pansler."

"Pansler stupid-ass. Hurt Hunter."

"Yeah, well --"

"He's sorry." Vivian reached out to Hunter. "He didn't mean to."

"First New, who you name?"

"I'm Vivian Towers. Vi-ve-en."

"Vivian want stupid-ass Pansler?"

The doctor shrugged, unsure of the appropriate response. If this was a test of tribal law, she should say no, but if it was a test of their friendship, she should be honest.

"Vivian, Pansler, mates." Hunter accepted her hand, but placed it on Pansler's left shoulder.

"Thank you." Vivian turned back to Hunter and signed 'same'. "Now we really are the same."

"Yes." Hunter nodded. "Find zoo. Find god-no-god. Much talk. Much ask. Much learn."

Chapter Eight
Cake

"Hunter Rogue, this is Munsi Arton." They were in the bio lab. Towers introduced the two who had known each other all Hunter's life.

Hunter was a little frightened. Maybe she was wrong. She did not want to seem timid now.

"Same," she signed it. "Hunter, Munsirtno, we same."

"Oh, my!" Munsi quickly repeated 'same' by signal and voice.

"Munsi," she corrected her mispronunciation. "Hunter, Vivia, Stupid-ass, Ribas, we same. No animal, no god."

'That's right. We're not animals and we're not gods. We are human." Vivian wrapped her arms across her chest in delight.

"I am not human. I am Bicanthran." Munsi pointed at his own chest and his ears purple with insult.

"Bicanthran? No same we?"

"Yes, same." Munsi looked at his four legs and two arms and sighed, "And not the same."

"Please." Hunter tried to control her emotions. Finding out your god was not a god, but an equal was very disturbing. Hunter experienced that lost and found feeling again. "Munsi -- same and same."

"Why couldn't her first question be 'why is the sky blue'?" Pansler whispered to Rivers.

"Stupid-ass no same!" Hunter curled her lip and took out her frustration on Pansler. "Go or no talk!"

"Yes, ma'am!"

"Munsi not god."

"I'm not a god," he agreed.

"Why eat babies? Why eat old ones? Same, same. Munsi eat Bikan-babies? Munsi eat Munsi-old-ones?"

"We don't eat your children!" Munsi was deeply hurt. "We care for you! We take care of you! We raised you! We feel great -- affection --"

"Much time -- Hunter, animal, same. In here."

Hunter touched her chest. "Much time, Munsi god in here." She tapped her forehead.

"Much time, god eat babies, god eat old ones, god eat talk ones. Yes!" Hunter's anger was beginning to show. "Much time I see! Gods no see Hunter. Hunter good. Hunter smart. Munsi no eat. Munsi-same-gods yes eat. I see much times!"

Munsi sank to the floor, folding his four legs beneath him, and put his head in his hands.

"Why?" Hunter touched his shoulder.

"I don't know. I didn't know. I'd heard rumors, but . . ."

"No!" Hunter grabbed his chin and pulled his face up to meet her eyes. "Munsi, Hunter, same! No see down. See Hunter! Tell Hunter!"

The Bicanthran began to shake and cry. "Because, my dear Hunter Rogue, to us, you were just animals."

Hunter patted his head and nodded. "To us, same." She pointed to the screen focused on her troop. "This, animals. No human."

"Hunter, we need your help. We need to make your people understand that they are not animals. Help them understand they are humans." Vivian stood next to her.

"No god talk dark."

"What?"

"No -- human talk -- dark sleep."

"Don't play the linguistic -- the talking tapes at night?" Vivian exclaimed.

"Same! Yes!"

"Hunter, they have to learn to speak."

"Speak human, yes. No speak god."

"I don't understand."

"Let me try. When you hear talk at dark when you sleep, you thought it was god." Rivers pantomimed each verb and noun.

"Riba Male smart."

Rivers grinned. Pansler curled his top lip.

"But your people will kill you if you talk." Vivian ignored her colleagues.

"Yes."

"What do you want to do?" asked Rivers.

"Damn smart! You mate Face, yes?" Hunter laughed at his expression. She understood their prejudice a little, now. She had not realized how Angus might react if he ever found out who she was -- before.

Hunter walked through the door into the room

her people shared. She bowed deeply to Bigfeet and then went to her friend Face. 'Same,' she signed. She walked to Notoes and signed 'same'. One more sign to Redears, then Hunter walked back to the door. 'Come,' she signed. They followed, curious.

The bio lab was a shock to the three unmated females, but the hallway was even greater. The females clung to each other, cooing gently.

Hunter walked to the panel she recognized in the wall. She touched a button and said very distinctly, "Cake."

Her friends growled.

Hunter let them taste the dark, rich chocolate. They liked it and signed for more.

"Cake," she said again, letting them each take another bite. This time, their growls weren't so fierce.

She ordered another cake, this time saying 'cake' as each female took a bite. When it was gone, they signed for more. Hunter pressed the button, but waited.

'More!' they signed. Hunter touched her fingers to her lips and nodded. The females backed away, frightened, but terribly tempted.

"Ka!" The syllable shot out of Face's mouth; the

others shoved her away from them. Hunter whispered into the wall and handed the entire portion to Face. The others watched with agitated envy as their friend swallowed great gulps of the delicious new food. Face did not share.

After Face's second helping, the other two looked at each other, and then said together, "Ka-ka!"

While they gorged themselves, Hunter spoke the word, "harp' at the wall and the hall was filled with her Angus' favorite music.

From there on, the three females were voracious learners. Two weeks passed before Hunter felt they were ready for the final step.

She assembled her females and the doctors in front of the computer one morning. Pressing the pastel pink button, she stated, "Star room. Where find."
A map was quickly displayed. The doctors became the navigators, but after an hour, they finally arrived at the observation deck anyway.

Angus was not there as Hunter had hoped. She had not seen him during these two weeks and she hurt inside.

"We are not animals. We are not gods. We are human." Hunter was proud of the speech she had been practicing. She pressed the wall and exposed the myriad lights of the universe to awaken her friends to their selves.

Tears rolled down her cheeks. She slipped quietly from the room, unnoticed.

She found his room easily, but he was not there. The room was neat and tidy, nothing in it was changed, but she felt so different.

She sprayed his scent onto her wrists, but touched nothing else. She walked through his quarters, labeling many items that had been mysterious to her only two weeks before.

She still had much to learn.

She heard the door swish open, but was afraid to face him. Would he see her as a human? Would he know who she was and what she had been?

"Untar?" His voice trembled.

"Angus." Her courage failed her. "Angus. I am Hunter Rogue." She pronounced the 'h'. "I live much time in zoo."

She heard him walk closer. She heard the breath he drew in. "I know. I found out after you left."

"Angus say,' Hunter go, Angus die.' Angus say,

'Live in zoo, die.' Hunter say," she turned to face him. "Angus hate Hunter, Hunter die."

"Angus --" The captain drew himself together and started again. "I don't hate you, Untar. I missed you very much." He took a step closer.

"I hurt." Hunter pointed to her chest. "Here."

"I hurt here, too." Angus pointed likewise. "It's called love. I love you. You love me."

"Please, Angus!" She wiped a tear from his cheek. "I stay with you all time. Please. No go. Mate all time. Make babies. Make hurt go."

"God, Untar. I can't --" He buried his face in her hair and embraced her. "You can't possibly understand, and I can't think how to explain it to you. You are a Katargan. You're one of the richest women in the galaxy. I have a few months before I retire. You have your whole life ahead of you. I have the last tail end of mine."

She was sobbing. His words were incoherent. All she heard was his rejection.

"You say 'not hurt'. You say!" She pushed away from him and ran into the passageway.

He did not follow.

Chapter Nine
Pregnant

Captain McFarlane signed off the bio lab's requisition for extra housing, keeping a mental note of the room number. Hunter Rogue refused to live in the zoo anymore. She had asked for a place of her own.

"Can talk. I not animal. No live zoo. Die if live zoo."

Vivian offered to share her quarters, but this angered Hunter. "Vivian, Hunter not same. Vivian see Hunter in zoo. Hunter want --" she passed her hand over her forehead, down to her chin, and across her shoulder.

"You want to forget the zoo?"

"Maybe yes. Maybe no time 'forget'."

Hunter liked her room. It was small, with room enough for a couch, a food console/computer table, and a bed.

Hunter spent her days teaching her students.

There were nine of them now. After being exposed to the observation deck, each female had chosen two others to accompany them the next day. Hunter's lessons consisted of naming items around them. Most of the verbs they learned were necessary, basic actions: eat, talk, have, see, hurt, like. What Hunter did not know, she asked about. If no one around her knew, she made it up.

She was a strict teacher and sometimes lost her patience. What made sense to her and followed logically along what she had already learned sometimes remained vague to her friends. She could not understand why some concepts so simple to her would be so difficult to others.

The others still slept in the communal room. They remained silent there, and kept up the traditions of their troop.

Hunter spent her evenings exploring the 'ship'. She learned to work the console and sometimes asked questions of it. It showed her graphs, maps, pictures, diagrams, and objects that she could understand. The strange white designs on the black background intrigued her. Angus 'read' these marks. She wanted to know more about them, but Vivian was busy with the silent animals still in the zoo. Rivers was helping her with the new humans, but only during the day. And she still hated Pansler. She did not ask for Munsi's help. He felt uncomfortable around her. There was no one else to ask. She refrained from becoming friends with any more 'crew'.

The 'read' marks were a challenge. She would learn it, but not right now. She started going to bed early, strangely exhausted. Her dreams were filled with memories of the zoo. She tossed and turned, sometimes crying out in her sleep. Her appetite declined, she felt sickened by the sight or smell of certain food.

Sometimes, she caught Vivian or Rivers watching her. They wore concerned expressions. They did not think to tell her of Captain McFarlane's visits. Angus made sure she never saw him. He asked for weekly reports and had all videos piped up to his quarters.

Then one day, Hunter stood up too fast and fainted. The doctors gave her a thorough examination. They held a conference to discuss the findings.

The four doctors visited Hunter's quarters late that evening. She welcomed them, ordered coffee for everyone, and listened to what they had to say.

"Hunter, you're going to have a baby." Vivian had been elected spokeswoman. "Do you understand?"

"I am mated. Mated ones have babies."

"You're going to have a baby soon."

"Yes?" She caressed her slightly swollen tummy.

"Hunter, it's not Uri's baby. He can't have children."

"Because he hurt me." Hunter nodded knowingly. They all glared at Pansler.

Uri grimaced. "I didn't mean to hurt you. You were a virgin. It always hurts women their first time. I didn't hurt you on purpose, honest. And it wasn't like it was my idea. Anyway, I'm sorry."

"Sorry, too. Bite you, you mated with Vivian. I not know, not see. Think animal. Have strong -- Damn!" She peered at them through the layers of her traditions. "Mated ones strong. Not mated, have no strong. Not same. I want have strong. I want same Bigfeet. You one male not mated. I see 'not mated' shoulder. I think Hunter get strong, mate Second New."

Munsi interrupted, "Second New?"

"My word for Pansler. Vivian, First New."

"Hunter," Vivian took her hand. "Who is your

mate?"

Hunter squeezed her hand and hung her head. "Have no mate."

"You must have one. Pansler is not your mate. He can not make a baby in you."

"Have baby now. No need mate."

"But Hunter, you needed a mate to make a baby. You needed a mate to --"

Again Munsi spoke, "Who made the baby with you?"

Hunter shrugged.

"You don't know his name?" Pansler asked.

"Hunter, did he hurt you?" Vivian spoke gently.

She nodded. "Hurts much. Hurts all time. Hurt no go. Hurt stays in here." A tear fell as she pointed to her heart.

"Oh, Hunter!" Vivian hugged her.

"Wouldn't you like to tell him you're going to have a baby?" Pansler spoke softly.

"Why?"

"Well, uh, because . . ."

"I ask. Hunter live all time. Make babies. Love all time. He say no."

"Bastard!"

Hunter laughed. "That he say about you! He say, 'Bastard ottabe kastard.'"

"You've told him about us then, about you? Does he know who you are? Is that why you think he said no?" Vivian smiled reassuringly.

"No and yes. We same. We see, we talk, we laugh, we touch, we make babies. Much happy. Much learn!"

Hunter sipped her coffee, trying to form her words. "Time, I am animal in zoo. I look, see, find, learn. I meet Angus. Good time. Best time. Time, I know I human, not animal, not god. I come here. Time, I go see him. Tell him, 'I am Hunter Rogue.' He know zoo. He hate zoo. He hate Hunter Rogue."

"Oh no. He just doesn't understand. We'll teach him to understand." Pansler touched Hunter's knee, consoling her.

"Don want teach him. He say 'Angus no hurt.' Angus yes hurt! All times, all times much hurt. What is word -- say no, do yes?"

"Lie?" Munsi offered.

"Angus lie." Hunter assimilated the new word. "Angus say want Hunter-me. Angus say touch-good me. Angus say love me. Now Angus see me, see animal-human me."

"Angus?" Rivers spoke for the first time.

"First see, I name him 'No Hair Male Leader'. Not can say words, but know name."

"Dear God, it can't be!" Rivers put his hands over his face.

"Who? Why?" Pansler was frightened.

"Captain Angus McFarlane."

Vivian quickly keyed something into the computer; a biography, accompanied by a picture appeared before them. "Hunter, is this the father of your baby? Is this Angus?"

Hunter stroked the surface of his face. "Angus."

"Oh, God, we're dead. We are dead!" Rivers whined.

"Angus not god. Angus not eat us."

"That's what you think!" Rivers whispered under his breath.

Pansler jumped up and began to pace. "What the hell are we supposed to do now?"

"Hunter, does Angus know you're going to have a baby?" Munsi's calm voice helped settle the others.

Hunter was confused. "We mated."

"Yes, well, sometimes that doesn't always --"

Pansler began his annoying rambling. "I mean, we 'cave men', crew men, you understand 'we'? We can choose to -- How am I supposed to explain this?!"

"What my mate is trying to say is, Angus may not know you are pregnant. Did you tell him with words that you were pregnant?"

"No?" Hunter looked from one expression to the next, all were different. "One time talk have baby. Angus say no. Last time I see him."

"Did you ask him or did you tell him?"

"Ask, tell, same."

"No, it isn't, dear." Munsi scratched himself behind the ear. "Not at all."

"We need to talk about this. She doesn't understand!" Pansler's fear suddenly turned to anger.

"For once, I agree with you." Rivers drummed his fingers on the console. "We're supposed to be repatriating them. It would be hard enough adjusting them to our way of life, but they've got to fit in and be accepted by the Katargans. We just barely have their word of honor not to execute them for two years -- until they've been made to understand their 'Role in God's Destiny'. If we present an unwed mother to them -- the others aren't exactly 'married in the sight of God', but at least they've been through a monogamous ceremony of sorts."

"Why scared? What bad?"

Rivers jabbed a finger at Hunter. "Listen to her! In her mind she's done nothing wrong. Hell and damnation, in our minds, she's done nothing wrong! But they'll put her to death before the Katargans would even listen to us. Not only her, but us, too. And Captain McFarlane! We all signed that 'Covenant of Responsibility'."

"Should have thought about that before you let her wander around those air vents."

"ME? I told you no, Pansler! I told you to check with the Captain first!"

"No talk!" It was the first time in her life she had shouted. "OUT! Go out! No talk. Hunter much -- I am much tired. I sleep. Out go."

They filed out, silently defeated.

Hunter turned back to the view screen and stroked the image of Angus. She ran her fingers over the 'read' marks. "Must read," she said to herself.

"Do you wish the text to be read?" the voice in the table asked.

"Yes, read!" She sat and listened. The computer

read the entire biography on Angus. It took two hours, he was that outstanding a man. She understood very little of it, but she knew how to get more information now.

The text ended. Hunter touched the screen again. "Hunter Rouge. Read."

The voice began again as the visual switched. The picture of her was taken before she came on the ship. She looked wild, fierce, an animal. She did not know it, but Munsi Arton himself had taken that picture. He used it on the cover of his best-selling book, Laughing Humans on the Brink of Extinction. That of course was before he published his theory The Origin of Laughing Humans -- Galactic Visitors to Our World, and the end of an otherwise brilliant career.

Her bio was short. It cited her adaptability and listed all of her intelligence and aptitude test results. "Believed to be a descendant of the Lost Tribe of Katarga, Hunter Rogue is enroute to the planet Datavista VII to be repatriated." Her bio ended.

"Katarga, planet Datavista Seven. Read."

The text on Katarga was beyond her. The words and concepts were too advanced. She fell asleep before it ended, and the voice droned on in her dreams. As with her 'conversations with god', her mind developed an idea of what the words might mean.

Katarga was a troop led by females. They spoke only when their conversation was about god. They had many rules, all punishable by death.

"All property of a prisoner reverts to the church in the case of his or her execution.' This phrase hung in her memory, haunting her while she slept. She understood none of the words, but she knew it was a terrible thing. Much strong.

She woke up sweating.

Chapter Ten
Bigfeet

All ten of the unmated women and two of the children spoke now. It was time to shake her troop's traditions to the foundations. The doctors wanted to take the men out of the communal room. They did not understand. Hunter would just have to show them.

She pulled on her outfit and walked to the mirror. Vivian said she was 'three months' now. Computer read to her all about 'pregnant'. She knew what her baby looked like by the pictures and diagrams that went with the text.

"Hunter! Come! Help!" Face ran into her room and grabbed Hunter by the arm. She had run through the halls naked.

"Come! Come!"

Hunter ran with her back to the communal room. The troop were all standing, slapping their bodies. Fear and sweat tinged the air. Children were crying. The males were gathered in the center. The females looked up at Hunter as she walked in. They quieted, waiting for her leadership.

She scanned the room again and gasped. Grabbing Face's arm, she whispered fiercely, "Where's Bigfeet? Where's Female Leader?"

"Old one dead. No make babies," she whispered back.

"Where?"

Face pointed at the all too familiar air vent.

Darkarm clapped his hands. He walked to Hunter, waiting.

"I am Hunter Rogue. I am human. We are human." She had to raise her voice above the growls. The mated and unmated females quickly divided, the ones who could speak came closer to Hunter. "You see stars. Gods no eat babies. Gods no eat talkers. Gods no eat old ones."

One of the mated females broke through the crowd and struck Hunter, knocking her backwards. Darkarm flung himself over her, protecting her from any further attack.

Suddenly everyone was talking at once. Those who did not know words, howled. In the confusion, Hunter and Darkarm slipped into the air vent and went in search of Bigfeet.

They silently followed her scent through the vents. Bigfeet had kept mostly to the main vents. Occasionally, she turned right. For hours, the couple tracked her. They could tell where she had rested, and they hoped to overtake her.

Bigfeet would keep traveling until she could go no farther. There, she would lay down and allow herself to die. All females knew this. It was their responsibility.

Hunter remembered when her mother left to die. Hunter was still a child. She had no brothers or sisters. Her mother's mate had been taken by the gods -- No, Hunter corrected herself -- taken by the Bicanthran, three years earlier. He was sick. He coughed all the time and spit out blood sometimes. After that, her mother did not get pregnant. Even as a child, Hunter knew that having a mate and making babies were the same thing.

It was winter when her mother left. She gave Darkarm to Bigfeet that morning. Then she smiled at

Hunter, turned her back on her troop, and walked away.

It was cold. The snow on the ground was etched by the ceaseless wind. When her mother had not returned after two days, Hunter left to find her. It was her first excursion. In her desperation, she wandered the perimeters of her world and discovered it was a cage.

It was so important to Hunter to find Bigfeet. To tell her (and her mother) they had finally found their way out.

It seemed Bigfeet had also discovered this. Darkarm and Hunter tracked her scent as it turned off to the left for the first time. At the end of the tunnel, the screen had been removed.

Darkarm had never been out of the communal room. He had been mated for twenty years, so he had not left the troop in all that time.

"Bathroom." Hunter identified where they were. "See: toilet, sink."

Darkarm nodded, then sniffed. He pointed to the door. She showed him how to open it and they walked through.

The corridor was empty this late in the evening.

They sniffed again and both headed left.

Hunter was feeling dizzy. She had not eaten all day, nor had anything to drink. She paused at a food console and ordered, "Two total pizza, two apple juice."

Her companion nibbled it cautiously, then tore into it with glee. "Good food!" he mumbled around a mouthful.

"You can talk!"

"Yes, yes," he slurped down the juice. "Talk in sleep. Learn much."

"Why not talk?"

"Do talk. Talk to Mate."

"Bigfeet can talk?"

"Yes. Not much. Babies. Food. Yes. No." Darkarm jabbed the buttons. "Two ottl pet-za. Puljuc."

The console opened to provide the food.

"We walk. We must find mate."

"You need clothes."

"Why?"

Hunter thought deeply, trying to convey the concept into words. "Crew females not see scar. See all of you. Maybe want Darkarm for mate."

"Hunter?" He stopped and looked at the floor. "Crew females have mates?"

"Yes. Show not same. No scar. Vivian and Pansler mates."

"Have much mates? Two? Three?"

"I not know."

"You?" He glanced up and frowned.

"Have one mate."

"Second New." He growled.

"No, Second New is Pansler. First New is Vivian. I not know. No scar. No words to make know."

"Hunter," he looked into her eyes. All of the unspoken feelings they had always shared were expressed in his face. "If no find mate, Hunter touch me."

"We find Bigfeet. We talk no time "Hunter touch you.' I have mate. His name Angus, Ship Leader. I have baby, here." She rubbed her abdomen.

A tear glistened on Darkarm's cheek. It ran down into his thick black beard. She caressed his jaw. "I'm sorry."

A crew female screamed. She had just turned into the hallway and was startled by the sight of a two-meter tall, naked, hairy man.

Hunter took Darkarm's hand and they ran the other way.

Dressed in a gray outfit that brought out the silver strands in his hair, Darkarm picked up his mate's scent again and led Hunter toward an elevator.

The door shut on them and opened again.

"Room no same!" Darkarm yelled and backed into the wall.

"No. This room go up, down, right, left, fast-fast."

"Where find Mate go?"

"I don't know." Hunter shook her head. She remembered being lost for hours in this very room.

"Destination, please." The soft elevator voice startled both of them.

"Observation deck," Hunter annunciated.

She watched Darkarm's reaction to the stars and realized how similar he and Angus were.

She knew how to get back to her quarters from the Obdeck. They were home within an hour.

"Good room. Soft chair. Good smell." Darkarm settled on the couch. "Pizza?"

"No. Cake. Coffee." She pressed the proper controls. As it delivered her favorite foods, she got an inspiration.

"Map. Ship!" she commanded the computer. It displayed the cylinder with notations: 60 kilometers long by 40 kilometers in diameter.

"Specify quadrant and sector," the voice said.

"Where find Bigfeet?" Hunter hoped it would be that simple.

"Bigfeet is not listed. Please specify or try again.

"Bigfeet. Mate of Darkarm. Leader of Zoo."

The computer remained silent.

Darkarm tried, "Big. Female. Much old. Three children. Brown fur. Brown eyes."

"Incomplete data." The computer shut off. Hunter knew it had little patience. Three mistakes and the voice went away.

Her cabin door swished open, silhouetting a man in the frame.

"Untar. May I come in?"

"Angus!" She leapt up and ran to him.

"Oh, I'm sorry. I didn't know you had -- I mean -- You have a man -- company. I'll leave."

"Angus stay! Angus help. Must help find Bigfeet. This Darkarm, Bigfeet-Mate." She pulled him into the room. Darkarm stood, recognizing the name, and glared at his rival.

"What's wrong?" The huge bearded man made Angus nervous. "Calm down and tell me."

"Sit." The men bristled on the couch, Hunter sat on the floor facing them. "Female leader Bigfeet go out Zoo. Go in air tunnel. Go in ship. Go die because old, no make babies. We look -- no find. Must find she. This," Hunter brushed her hand over the computer. "This know much. Tell much. Read much. Show much. You know how tell -- how ask. Yes? Ask yes asks, this voice tell me, show me where find."

"How could the computer isolate your leader?"

"She touch, she eat, she take. Cave - no - crewmen see Bigfeet. Talk her. Know she --" Hunter looked to Darkarm, embarrassed. "Crewmen know she zoo animal, not ship human."

Captain McFarlane considered the logical questions and choices. "Computer. List any unusual reports as to the theft of clothing or other items, reports citing unusual personnel, inexperienced use of elevators, lifts, and comp consoles. Date effective -- wait." He looked at Hunter. "How long has she been missing? Much time? One, two, three darks?"

"Morning, this day." She was showing off her vocabulary.

"Computer continue. Date effective one solar day."

The console displayed the information.

"Show where. On map." Darkarm spoke to Angus, but the computer took it as a command and plotted each incident on the ship's map.

"Isolate quadrant four, section D-five. Magnify." Angus spoke calmly while he watched Darkarm. He was impressed by Darkarm, but was choking on jealousy. He had always been a jealous man -- overly possessive of his ships and his women. Jealousy made him an outstanding captain, but a miserable lover. Who was this savage to Untar?

"Where we?" Darkarm crouched over the table. A light pulsed on the location of Hunter's cabin. "Where bathroom screen down?" Again the light pulsed. "Where Zoo?"

"Specify."

"Indicate the quarters of the Katargan colonists," McFarlane rephrased.

Darkarm traced the path, intuitively following their search that day. Then his finger returned to the pulsing bathroom. As he traced Bigfeet's path, he explained. "First clothes." He traced the hallways to the incidence of a stolen blue outfit. It was marked on the map by a representation of the missing item. "Second, food." He followed the 'comp error' marks. "See people. Scare and yes-no hurt." He traced over the stick figures. "Learn fast. Look same." The path he traced disappeared, no more strange incidents.

"She could learn that quickly, in a day?"

"We smart. Must needs be." She looked into his eyes and again felt her heart race. He felt the same way. She had lived her life communicating by facial expressions. She read his face as easily as he read a book.

"She no talk much." Darkarm wanted to interrupt this visual exchange.

"Oh, I think Untar says everything that needs to be said." His voice was soft and gentle, like the first time she met him.

"Darkarm-I have much hair!" Bigfeet's mate stood up, letting his emotions carry him. "You baby -- have hair?"

"What the devil?"

"Darkarm, sit! No speak!"

"Angus. You mate Hunter. You make strong babies?"

"Darkarm. No speak. Angus not know."

"Angus not know you have baby? Why mate

Angus? Mate me! Make babies we! Make strong babies. Bigfeet babies no strong. No smart. Hunter, Darkarm babies much smart!"

  She ran from the room. She could not face them both. She felt very sick and very tired, but she just kept running.

Chapter Eleven

Linguistic Revolution

Captain Angus McFarlane stood on the observation deck, staring at the universe for more than three hours. She never came. He was so sure this was where he would find her. He had made a lot of mistakes in his life. Somehow, he felt this was his worst.

He walked silently into his quarters. Their emptiness overwhelmed him. He let his clothes fall to the floor and crawled into bed.

"I like watch you undress."

"Untar!" He swallowed her in his arms.

He breathed against her hair, she pressed her face against his curly chest.

"Captain Angus McFarlane. You listen me good. I no ask, I tell. Angus touch me. Angus kiss me. Angus make me see stars here this bed. I no ask, I tell." She held both sides of his face. "You hear me, Angus?"

"Yes!" He laughed. "Yes, I hear -- Angus hear Hunter."

They began to giggle and kiss and touch and their breath came in gasps. They did not hear the door open. They were oblivious to the sound of feet walking across the padded floor.

"What they do?"

"Dear God!" Angus touched on the lights.

"They mate, see?" A huge, hairy-faced man pointed at Hunter and Angus.

"Not how mate." A huge, dark-haired woman looked confused.

"Bigfeet!" Hunter sprang from the bed and embraced her. "Darkarm find you!"

"What you do with male?" Bigfeet was disappointed the hairless male had covered himself with the bedclothes.

"We make baby." Hunter smiled and pulled her leader into the living room. She ordered chocolate cake, coffee, pizza, and apple juice for everyone. Angus joined them, wrapped in a robe. He draped another robe over Hunter's shoulders.

Bigfeet pulled at the bottom corner of Angus' robe, trying to peek at him.

"Stop that!" Angus snatched his robe away from her fingers.

Bigfeet had never seen a dominant male. And to be commanded to do something by him --! She growled.

"Bigfeet." Hunter stood and tied the robe around her. "We must needs clothes. See? Cover all ones."

"Why?" Bigfeet was still angry.

"You see him, you want mate him. He Hunter-mate, but no scar. You not know, make big bad." Darkarm enjoyed being able to explain things to his mate.

"No Hunter-mate. Other New Male Hunter-mate. I know this."

"We make big bad." Hunter faced the floor and spoke softly. "New Female, New Male mates. No scar, not know. Make big bad."

Bigfeet, as well as Angus, contemplated this.

"Coffee?" Hunter offered a mug to Angus.

"No." Angus touched the console. "Whiskey, neat."

"How find Bigfeet?" Hunter asked, disturbed by

Angus' expression.

"See map. See map 'here'." Darkarm pointed to his head. "Go find last mate-touch. There, Darkarm-I smell Mate. Go find Mate. She in room much much old ones. Much old Mate, not much old Angus." Darkarm was pleased he had insulted Angus. He continued, "No can mate with clothes. Much laugh old ones. We happy. Much laugh Darkarm, Darkarm-mate."

"But how did you find us?" Angus cringed, thinking about the reports he would have to initial tomorrow.

"Ask voice in wall."

"What did you ask the computer?"

"Darkarm-I say, 'Captain Angus McFarlane, where find?' Wall show map. Keep map 'here'," again he pointed to his head. "Find Captain Angus McFarlane and Hunter Rogue. We watch much time."

"You what?" Angus decided to order another whiskey.

"Not know if you hurt Hunter. Make talk -- 'oo, ah, yes!' Hurt -- yes, no?" Bigfeet commented.

"No, not hurt. Not hurt no time!" Hunter's eyes sparkled.

"Do this, make baby?" Her mate had told her Hunter was pregnant.

"Make baby good." She smiled at Angus, who turned a strange pink color. "Best."

"Show. Hunter, Angus show Leader-I, Leader-mate how make baby best."

"The hell I will!" Angus stood, his ears were scarlet.

The three colonists whispered between themselves, very confused.

"They have not shut up all night long. Hunter, Darkarm, and Bigfeet have not come back. A Katargan delegation from Datavista VII is due to intercept us within a week. And I just don't know what to do!" Rivers put his head between his hands and sobbed.

"It was a linguistic revolution!" Munsi explained to Vivian, who had been there the whole time herself. "We've recorded all thirty hours of it. Those who are awake are still talking."

"It seems that once they realized it was permissible to speak, they made up for lost time. Their rate of assimilation is astronomical!" Pansler made computer adjustments.

"I think Hunter had the key all the time -- stars -- 'astronomical'!" Munsi shook his head in awe.

Towers crossed her arms thoughtfully. "I would have thought the power of verbal communication had atrophied, like our appendix. But obviously, they continued to think in phonemes. When we enhanced and reinforced these concepts with our subliminal linguistics, we thought we were being ineffective. But all it took was an emergency to bring it all to the surface, overriding their taboo and traditions."

Munsi patted Towers on the bottom as a reward for her perception. He rather enjoyed this erotic foreplay to which she was ignorant.

"In a sense, the emergency caused them to regress to a state prior to their concept of a punishing god," Munsi theorized.

"Yes, that was it!" Pansler innocently patted Munsi's shoulder, startling the Bicanthran. Munsi was not attracted to males.

"Or they've advanced beyond it." Vivian licked her lips.

"Oh, dear God. That Katargan delegation is going to flail the skin right off our bones!" They looked questioningly at Rivers. "The Katargans still believe in a punishing god."

"Angus?" Hunter whispered so as not to wake the two people on the floor. "What mean 'execute'?"

"Execute?" Angus snuggled closer to her. "Execute means to do something, to put it into effect. Like "I execute the command.'"

"How execute a female?"

"A female? Oh, to execute someone means to kill them for political reasons. If someone breaks a rule, the government may execute her, kill her for her crimes."

He felt her tense against him.

"Don't worry. We don't execute people anymore."

"Angus, Katargan, not same?"

"God, no!"

"Katargan execute female. Execute babies."

He felt her pull away and sit up.

"Yes, the Katargans still execute some of their followers." He reached for her, took her trembling hand. "How do you know about the Katargans?"

"Voice in table."

"And what have you learned?"

"We must needs be Katargan. We must needs go Datavista. Is true?"

"It is believed," he pulled her back into his arms. "That you are descendants -- children of children of children -- of a Katargan ship. If this is true, you will all be extremely wealthy."

"What means 'wealthy'?"

"Rich! All the money, food, clothes, things you ever want."

"Have all things this time."

"Oh, my darling! There is wealth, and there is Wealth! You could have so much more."

"Where wealth -- where Katargan find wealth?"

"I don't know. They are the most powerful church in the Alliance."

"Voice in table say wealth from execute."

He didn't comment.

"Angus, tell me -- god kill babies?"

"No, He doesn't."

"Bad kill. Bad execute. Bad wealth."

"It's a little more complicated than that."

"I must needs know more."

Hunter spent days listening to the computer

records about Katarga. When her brain stopped at the brink of exhaustion, she asked the voice to read to her from the Bible. She slept fitfully and dreamed of being caught in the fire tunnel again.

Bigfeet and Darkarm returned to the communal room and led their people toward verbal freedom. They all seemed to pit themselves against ignorance and silence. The room constantly rang with voices, words, syllables, songs, and much laughter.

The colonists' language developed rapidly. Within a week, all twenty-seven of them (except the two infants), could identify hundreds of nouns and verbs and were becoming creative with adjectives and adverbs. They wandered the halls and made friends with most of the crew they met. The unmated females went wild! Their possibilities were astounding.

They made quite a lot of mistakes. But they were learning to learn. Once that gap was bridged, Munsi knew the Laughing Humans of Bicanthra III would never be silent again.

Chapter Twelve

Laughing Humans

The Katargan delegation docked their ship in the landing bay. They were escorted by the ship's security detail to the colonists' communal room. The colonists stood, watching the silent women dressed in red.

One woman stepped forward. She was younger than Hunter, but her face and body were hideously swollen. Hunter had seen the look before: she found a dead warneal one time, its body had been swollen like that. When Hunter prodded it with her spear, the warneal had burst open, spilling maggots and putrid slime all over the ground. But this Katargan was not dead. Hunter searched her vocabulary and found the proper adjective: fat. Hunter quelled her vivid imagination and paid attention.

"In the name of God, I welcome our children home. Who of you speak for God?"

"I am Leader. I am Bigfeet."

The Katargan glared up at her. "It is not the Will of God to be unproductive. One as old as you can not possibly be fruitful and multiply to the Glory of God's Universe. Therefore, I, Her humble servant, will not waste time by listening to you. There must be another of you who will speak to the Glory of God."

"Hunter." Darkarm understood. "Hunter Rogue will speak."

"If our Blessed Savior had wanted men to speak, She would have made them intelligent." The Katargan scowled at Darkarm's insolence.

"I am Hunter Rogue. I will speak." Hunter had dressed in a bright green suit. Her hair was shiny and clean. Her eyes had dark circles under them from her continuous studies.

"You are pregnant, Praise God." The Katargan nodded approval of Hunter.

"I am pregnant, praise Angus," she corrected her. Hunter smiled, slightly confused by the security detail's laughter.

"I see that, in God's wisdom, She has permitted a

slight language barrier between us. However, we will proceed, trusting in God's benevolence to lend insight to this unworthy servant." The Katargan seemed to sing these words. "I am Sister Obedience, Templar of the Holy Order of Katarga. It would Honor God to meet these sisters."

Hunter had to concentrate to understand her.

'This is Bigfeet, our leader. Her mate, Darkarm. Her children Beebee, Chichi, Deedee. This is Fourfingers. Her mate, Climber. Her children Notoes, Face, her son Roundjaw. Roundjaw is mate of Puffy. Puffy's children Summer, Winter, Autumn, Spring, and baby Brighteyes. This is Tita."

(Munsi did not explain that the doctors had insisted on changing her name slightly.)

"Her mate, Scarleg. Tita have baby soon. We will name it Ship. This is Fang. Her mate Bowchest. Bowchest and my mother's mate were sons of same female. They have no children. All die when babies."

"It is sometimes God's will to teach us humility."

"Six more female: Flower, Redears, Swimmer, Birdbeak, Squint, and Goldie. They have no mates."

"An unproductive womb is the devil's workshop." Sister Obedience did not approve of them.

"This is Dr. Munsi Arton. He is from Bicanthra III."

The Templar sneered at the heathen.

"This is Dr. Lee Rivers. Dr. Uri Pansler, mate of Dr. Vivian Towers."

"I can see by your faces you do not know the Glory of the Living God. But our Grand Mothers prayerfully consented to your intrusion into these matters."

"This is my mate, Captain Angus McFarlane." Hunter's eyes shone with pride.

"Your mate?" Sister Obedience's sneer turned to quick anger. "Were you married in the eyes of God?"

"God sees all things."

"Praise God, you do know the glory!"

"Hunter-I know many things. Hunter knows god not kill babies. Hunter knows god know worth of old ones and not kill them. Hunter knows talk is good."

"I'm sure with training and God's guidance, you will quickly become a true servant of the Living God." Sister Obedience took her arm and led her to the door. "I guess it's too much to hope any of you have been baptized."

"We humans born, mated, have babies, die. What mean baptized?"

"God's word teaches us that all must be baptized, washed in the blood, cleansed of sin, in order to receive the blessings of heaven."

"Blessings of heaven means wealth?"

"Yes! Praise God, you are perceptive!" Sister Obedience squeezed Hunter's arm affectionately.

"Babies washed in blood when born."

"Well, yes," Sister Obedience hesitated. "Praise God."

"Wealth come from this blood?"

"No, dear child of God. Wealth comes from the sacrifice of her servants."

Hunter assumed sacrifice and execute meant the same thing. She stepped away from the Templar and took a deep breath.

"When we zoo animals, we know god. We know god execute babies, talkers, old ones, sick ones. Computer tell me Katargans execute babies, old ones, sick ones, wrong talkers. Yes? Is true?"

"It is sometimes the place of the Church's elders to discipline the body."

"True kill these?"

"Yes. We believe it is God's Will."

"When we come here, this ship, we learn many

things. We learn we not zoo animals, we humans. We learn Bicanthrans not gods. We lost god, we find us."

"In God's name, what are you saying?" The smile of acceptance was gone from her pudgy face.

"Katargans still think god kills babies, old ones, yes?"

The sister nodded.

"Hunter Rogue say we -- Laughing Humans -- we never be zoo animals again. I say you Katargans zoo animals. Only animals think God kills babies."

"Blasphemy!"

"Not blast females, blast god of Katarga."

"You will be put to death! The wrath of God shall visit you and the curse of God will be passed from your children to your children's children!"

At a signal from the captain, the security detail pulled small shiny objects from their belts and pointed them at the Katargan delegation.

Sister Obedience, Templar of the Holy Order of Katarga continued sputtering religious zeal.

"My wife has spoken. She has declared herself and her people to be different in doctrine from the Church of Katarga. You are not on Datavista VII now. You are on my ship, with my security pointing weapons at you. Your church has no jurisdiction here." He took Hunter's arm and walked towards the delegation. "Thank you so much for bestowing on us the joy of your presence. We quite understand how valuable your time is, the harvest being ripe. We will escort you to your ship."

"What now? What we do now?" Darkarm asked Hunter. They were having a celebration dinner. The doctors, the captain, several crewmen, and all of the colonists looked to her, waiting for her reply.

Hunter shrugged. "We live."

"It's not that simple," Pansler sighed.

"No. I would imagine my retirement will be moved up several months." Angus gritted his teeth.

"We'll be lucky to be accepted as floor sweepers on Sand Dune Isle now." Rivers patted Pansler's leg.

"Why not come back to Bicanthra III with me? You could teach us so much!" Munsi spoke to Vivian.

"Are you sure your people would accept us?"

"No, Vivian, but your life won't be in danger as it is now from the Katargans."

"What do you two think?" she asked.

"I'd love it!" Pansler smiled.

Rivers looked down. "I think 'two's company, three's a crowd'."

"It wasn't a crowd last night." Vivian touched Rivers' chin.

"Really?"

"It was wonderful," Pansler tousled his hair.

Hunter looked up at Angus, confused by this new concept. He laughed.

"I was given a small moon for straightening out a dispute between two planets. There's plenty of room there. I never considered living there before, it was too lonely." Angus looked at the innocent faces before him. "I would be honored if you came to live with me. You unmated females are welcome to invite a crewman or two as well."

"We come. You teach us how make babies best." Bigfeet grinned.

"Well --" Angus turned pink as Hunter laughed. "We'll see."

E J R

ABOUT THE AUTHOR

Evelyn Rainey has had four novels published by traditional small press publishers in the last four years:

Minna Pegeen ISBN 978-1935361381
Comfort Publishing 2011
Bedina's War ISBN 978-1936695881
ASIN B00DVR2B7O Comfort Publishing 2012
Perky's Books & Gifts ISBN 978-1939065377
ASIN B00H75DOY0 Bedlam Press 2013
The Island Remains ISBN 978-1633557437
ASIN B00LGJ77ZK Whiskey Creek Press 2014
She edited and has a short story in **Stories for All Seasons**
ASIN B013FBFK4Q 2015.

A frequent guest author and panelist for Science Fiction/Fantasy conventions and writers conferences, she also writes the Science Fiction/Fantasy Books column for *BellaOnline* – the second largest women's emagazine in the world. Previously, she wrote the Veterans column for *BellaOnline* for three years. She has been published in *Zero Signal, Lakeland Ledger, Polk County Democrat*, **World Treasury of Golden Poems**, *Youth Alive, Wesleyan Magazine* and the Polk County Poetry Anthology. She is the owner of **Denouement Literary Agency, LLC**.

She worked at **Books-a-Million** for six years as a part-time paperback specialist and Red Badge. The experience has opened the door for her to hold book signings at **Books-a-Millions** throughout Florida. For ten years, she facilitated *Writers for All Seasons*.

Her online presence includes her website http://Evelyn-Rainey.com
Amazon Author page (amazon.com/author/evelynrainey)
Goodreads (goodreads.com/Evelyn_Rainey)
Facebook (EvelynRaineyAuthor)
Twitter (EvelynRainey)
as well as DenouementLit.com.

She has been an educator for thirty-two years. With degrees and certificates in Early Childhood, Elementary, Middle School Integrated Curriculum, Gifted, ESOL, and Journalism, she currently teaches Robotics and Spanish to gifted Middle School students at Jewett School of the Arts. Prior to that, she provided consultation for Gifted students and their teachers in traditional classrooms as well as alternative facilities including jails.

Outside of the school system, she is a Master Crocheter, equally conversant with traditional patterns and fine Irish Clones Crochet Lace and sells her handwork in her **Etsy.com** shop **TinkerLassie**. She is an herbalist, a singer, a belly-dancer and she loves to do book-signings.

Discussion Guide for Book Clubs

1. Value (What lessons were presented throughout the story? What lesson did you take away?)
2. Attitude (How closely did the attitude of the story itself match with your attitude about life?)
3. Authenticity (Were there any characters or situations which seemed very realistic or very unrealistic? How so?)
4. Point of View (Who told this story? Why?)
5. Cause & Effect (What was the initial event which caused the biggest motivation for the character and the plot to develop? Discuss the chain of events which were a direct effect of this cause.)
6. What if… (Find an event which, if it had not occurred, the major events would not have unfolded. How would the story have changed? How might it have stayed the same?)
7. Conflicts in characters (With whom does the main character have the most conflict? Within the main character, what are her conflicts? How are these resolved?)
8. Conflicts in setting (How does the setting – location, time, socio-ecological circumstances – create conflicts? How are these resolved?)
9. Conflicts along plot line (Where do the most conflicts arise? Are they all resolved by the denouement?)
10. Compare/contrast (Choose two characters or two major conflicts and compare how the author developed them. How are they alike? How do they differ? How would the story have been different if these two things were not developed in this fashion?)
11. Main idea established by title and book cover (When you first saw the cover and read the title, what were your thoughts about the main idea? Were those thoughts supported or changed over the course of reading the book? How so?)

12. Main idea established by values/morals (Do the values and the morals expressed in this book support the main idea? Conversely, does the main idea of this novel support the values and morals expressed?)

13. Main idea established by supporting details (Think of this book as a building. Which supporting details would be considered weight-baring so that if they were removed, the whole infrastructure would collapse?)

14. Genre – (What parts of the story are pure Science Fiction? What parts determine the subgenre Romance? How significantly would the story change if it were not this particular genre?)

15. Plot – Premise (What part of the premise drew you in and made you want to keep reading?)

16. Plot – Rising Action (Consider and discuss the pace of the rising action and developing conflicts.)

17. Plot – Climax (Was the climax what you expected? Were you satisfied by it or did you wish something else had happened?)

18. Plot – Falling Action (Consider and discuss the pace of the falling action and resolutions of the conflicts.)

19. Plot – Denouement (In what ways did the story's characters and conflicts end up? What was left unanswered? What had you wished happened differently?)

20. Validity and accuracy of information (What things were inaccurate or invalid?)

21. Flow and fluency of language (Quote three of your favorite parts of the story. Discuss the flow and fluency of the language used.)

ABOUT PORTALS PUBLISHING

What We Offer

- ✓ We publish in three versions: trade paperback, e-book and audio
- ✓ We distribute worldwide in English.
- ✓ We offer standard royalties for each of the versions based on net.
- ✓ We provide the book cover by a professional designer.
- ✓ We provide the author 10 copies as the advance.
- ✓ We post the author's discussion guide on the nation's largest book club database.
- ✓ We promote the book to the media (the author's local newspapers and radio stations) and the representative editor of the book's genre at BellaOnline (second largest women's e-magazine in the world)
- ✓ The author is responsible to do the research, but we will announce the book to as many groups for which the author can give us email addresses and/or meet-up contacts in the United States, Great Britain, Australia and New Zealand.
- ✓ We can help set up book signings and speaking/lecture tours.
- ✓ We will nominate the book for at least one, but possibly several literary awards throughout the contract's duration.
- ✓ We can help set up as much of the author's platform as the author wants – the author does the hard work; we'll assist and advise.
- ✓ We continuously assist the author with promotion strategies throughout the contract's duration.

PortalsPublishing.com
"The Best Books are Portals to a New World."

An imprint of **Denouement Literary Agency, LLC**
DenouementLit.com

You may also be interested in **Bliss Books**
BlissBooksOnliine.com
"Building Life-Long Inspirational & Successful Strategies"